Act Like you Love Me

Act Like you Love Me

CINDI MADSEN

Entangled Publishing, LLC
2614 South Timberline Road
Suite 105, PMB 159
Fort Collins, CO 80525
rights@entangledpublishing.com

Bliss is an imprint of Entangled Publishing, LLC.

Edited by Stacy Abrams and Alycia Tornetta
Cover design by Bree Archer
Cover photography by Artem Peretiatko/GettyImages

Manufactured in the United States of America

First Edition June 2013

Bliss

To everyone who's ever made a fool of themselves for love.

Chapter One

Working in a place where the clientele was 90 percent male should mean, statistically speaking, that Brynn would meet at least *one* guy who'd give her a hint of tummy butterflies. It'd been so long since she'd felt anything resembling attraction that she was afraid she might not recognize it anymore. Maybe those butterflies had died lonely deaths.

Maybe I'll *die a lonely death.*

"Got any of those bucktail jig kind?" the gentleman asked, never taking his eyes off the multicolored lures spread before him on the counter. Brynn had been so busy studying the way his white caterpillar eyebrows twitched, and how he had more hair coming from his ears and nose than he did on the top of his head, that it took her a couple of seconds to process the question.

She twisted the rotating stand and pointed to them. "These Conch Saltiga Jigs have been really successful lately from what I hear, so you might want to give them a try, too."

The man eyed them like he'd never seen anything so beautiful in his life. In fact, Brynn seriously considered asking if he needed a moment alone with them.

So, yes, a lot of men came into the Bigfish Bait and Tackle in Cornelius, North Carolina. But they were usually older and interested in things like chug bugs and live bait and the fishing pole that might make their trophy-fish-catching dreams come true.

Brynn rang up the man's purchases and then he took his bag and exited, the chime on the door sounding through the quiet. She glanced out the far window at Lake Norman, where the last rays of the day were dancing across the surface of the water. It was a pretty view, though she rarely got time to enjoy it from the outside these days. The TV to her left droned on, set to the World Fishing Network, playing a program she'd seen at least a million times already, give or take a few.

Her stomach growled and she put a hand over it. Paul had better get back with the food soon. Her brother had been gone for more than thirty minutes, and she was starting to consider the live bait in the fridge behind her as a viable dinner option.

What was taking him so long? He knew she had rehearsal soon, and with rush hour traffic it'd take longer to get to the theater in Charlotte. Knowing her brother, he'd probably gotten sidetracked—especially if his friend Wes had called and they'd started talking about adventure tour ideas or the band. Or sports. Paul swore he'd close up tonight, since she'd done it when the band played a last-minute show a couple of nights ago. If he didn't get here soon, she was never going to another one of his gigs. Actually, now that Wes was engaged to a cool girl and Brynn had someone to talk to during shows, that was a bluff. But next time, she was definitely doing the food run.

Brynn leaned across the display case and tapped her fingers on the glass. After a minute or so of that *exhilarating* activity, she grabbed two of the colorful rubbery fish still in their packages. She moved the bigger blue fish over to the bright yellow one, the plastic crinkling as she did. "Hey, swimming my way, hot stuff?" she asked in her best male fish voice.

Brynn circled the yellow fish away from the blue one, then folded it to do the mock-bashful glance back. "Of all the fish in the ocean, I only want you."

The blue fish zipped across to the yellow, their fishy faces met through the plastic, and—

The chime sounded, making Brynn jump enough that the fish flew up in the air before landing on the floor.

"What were you doing?" Paul asked, setting the brown sacks of heavenly, grease-scented food on the counter. "You look guilty."

Her family often teased her about her tendency to daydream, so no way was she going to admit to making two rubber fishing lures fall in love. "You took forever. Remember how I'm supposed to leave early?"

Paul was already unwrapping his burger and lifting it to his mouth. "Sorry. I ran into Rob and his family. And once I finally got to the diner, there was some new girl there, and she's *super slow*. I started to wonder if she had to head out back to kill the cow before she made our burgers."

Brynn tried to push away that image as she took a bite of her food—at this point it was cow or worms, so she was choosing the less-slimy option. "Okay, I'm eating on the run, then." She grabbed the bag, not willing to leave the French fries behind. "Catch you later."

"Break a leg," he called on her way out.

By the time she made the drive to the theater, she'd managed to get as much of her food on herself as in her mouth. "I swear, I'm such a mess," she muttered. Luckily, she was a *prepared* mess. She glanced around, then grabbed her spare shirt from the bag she kept behind the passenger seat.

Her heart quickened a bit as she got ready to make the switch.

Maybe I'll just wait and change inside. But she was already late, and then she'd have to take in her huge bag, and no one else parked behind the auditorium anyway. She yanked her shirt over her head. Of course the button got caught in her hair, because it was one of those kinds of days.

"Ouch, ouch, ouch." Pricks of pain dashed across her scalp as she pulled.

Finally she got it free, though there was a nice chunk of black hair around the yellow button.

She pulled on her spare shirt and flung open the door of her car—and noticed the guy standing nearby. He looked away, but he'd clearly gotten a show. Heat climbed up her neck and settled into her cheeks.

She'd like to say it was the first time she'd accidentally flashed someone. Hopefully between her car and tinted windows, she'd been partially hidden, but she still said a silent thank-you that she'd been wearing her cute pink bra. And at least it wasn't like back in high school when it'd been in front of an auditorium of people and her bottom half on display. Which was much, much worse, cute underwear or not.

Thinking of that moment must be making her see things.

Because… No… It couldn't be. The guy looked exactly like Sawyer Raines, the same guy she used to have the hugest, most embarrassing crush on. Back then, her list went something like: smokin' hot, completely oblivious she was alive, and so far out of her league it was more like another sport completely. Sawyer Raines had been all those things and then some, the guy all the girls wanted as their boyfriend, so of *course* she'd chosen him to obsess over.

And now she was staring at the Sawyer look-alike, and those butterflies she'd thought had died in her stomach long ago were flapping their sad, unused wings, attempting to fly. *Oh no. Bad idea, butterflies. That's a good way to get shot down.*

"Sorry," the Sawyer look-alike said, running a hand through his thick brown hair. "I was just passing by and…"

And saw me half naked. She tugged on the bottom of her shirt, like covering every inch now would make up for not having it covered a moment ago. That's when she noticed his eyes. Oh jeez. She'd once described them in her journal as two glowing emeralds, because she'd wanted to sound poetic, and who wouldn't want an emerald-eyed boyfriend, right?

It's him. Her pulse started climbing, and the flush was spreading faster and hotter. *And he just saw me in my underwear for the second time.*

All the awkwardness from high school came rushing back to her, twisting her stomach into a tight knot. She remembered being looked through like she wasn't there. Then being whispered about and laughed at, which had made her wish people would just go back to ignoring her. That awful nickname…

The crushing rejection from the very guy standing across from her. For a moment, she thought she might throw up, right there on the asphalt.

Sawyer extended his hand toward her. "Anyway, I'm—"

"I'm late." She charged toward the theater, head down. At least she was about to go pretend to be someone else for a while. Right now she thought it'd be nice to never be herself again.

• • •

So much for small-town charm, Sawyer thought, as he watched the woman walk away from him. But he supposed he was technically in Charlotte now. It was funny that driving thirty minutes from the lake made such a difference, but he swore people were more relaxed next to the water. He'd only been back in North Carolina for a week, but he'd been almost paranoid at first over how nice people were. Maybe five years in the Big Apple had changed him.

He missed the buzz of the city and his usual coffee cart. Missed walking down the street, lost in his thoughts. People here waved whether they knew you or not, and he felt so obligated to smile and engage in conversations he didn't have time for.

But Mom was right about finally doing something about the lake house. It was time to sell it and move on. Before they could list it, though, it needed serious renovations. Dad had taught him home repairs when he was younger, and even hired him to work summers at his construction company.

Until Dad couldn't work anymore.

The thought of someone else doing a project Sawyer had originally planned on doing with his dad turned his insides to lead, so he'd told Mom he'd come down and do the work.

He just didn't realize there'd be other strings attached. He sighed and headed toward the theater. He still couldn't believe he'd agreed to this. Actually, *agreed* wasn't really the right word. His aunt had guilt-tripped him to take over directing the play. He kept telling Aunt Wendy that he was a screenwriter, but she said he'd had theater classes and had dated an actress, and that made him more qualified than the person he was replacing.

If his aunt hadn't done so much for Mom the past few years, Sawyer would've refused. But he felt like he owed her. Enough to help put on this dinky play. According to Aunt Wendy, it was already cast, and rehearsals were well on their way. All he had to do was suffer through a month of practices and the actual putting on of the play. It should be wrapping up about the same time renovations would be completed, and then he'd be headed back to New York where he belonged.

He looked around the lobby—a tiny ticket booth and

an empty concession stand—and hiked up his laptop bag on his shoulder. This was supposed to be his writing time, so he was hoping everyone would direct themselves and he could sneak in an hour or so of work. Hell, maybe it'd even provide him with inspiration, something he'd been lacking lately. Everything he tried to write was total crap, and he was starting to rethink plots and even characters. Having one successful screenplay was making him overthink every detail of this one, and he was determined not to be a one-hit wonder.

As he walked into the auditorium, he took in the threadbare foldout seats, lights clamped onto the railing, and the large circular hanging stars and moons overhead.

Looks like I'll have to really stretch for inspiration here.

"Oh, Sawyer! There you are!" Aunt Wendy rushed up the maroon-carpeted aisle. She was short and squat and always running. And clapping. Like she was now. Very enthusiastic. He scolded himself for being such a jerk. Everything in his life was up in the air right now and it was making him grouchy.

I'll feel better once I start work on the house and get some scenes written. His mind was crowded with everything he needed to focus on. *Just got to prioritize.*

Above all, he wanted to sell the house for a good enough price for Mom to retire. So for now, he was a screenwriter slash renovations expert. Slash guy who was directing a local production of *The Importance of Being Earnest*, evidently. But he wasn't going to let the last one interfere with his two main goals.

Aunt Wendy led him front and center. The seats in the theater were so ancient that there was more spring than padding, and the one he sat in made a loud squeal as he settled into it. His aunt was listing everything that had been done, everything that still needed to be done, and talking so fast he wished he would've stopped for some kind of caffeinated beverage so he could keep up.

Aunt Wendy clapped. "Everyone! I've got an announcement! If you'll all gather round!"

People circled in from around the theater and several came out from behind the heavy maroon velvet curtains. Sawyer's attention was immediately drawn to the dark-haired girl in the middle of the stage. A few minutes ago he'd seen her changing in her car, struggling to pull off her shirt. She'd fought with it so long he thought he might have to go rescue her, but then she'd managed to get free. It wasn't like he'd seen much—okay, a sexy pink bra and lots of cleavage—but it had only taken her a few seconds to pull on her other shirt. He'd frozen in place, though, breath caught in his throat, his blood pumping double time. Then she was out of the car, and he'd stood there gawking at her like an idiot, no idea what to say. Especially when her cheeks colored and she blinked those beautiful hazel eyes at him.

Right now she was laughing with the guy next to her, the kind of joy-filled laugh that made him wish he were in on the joke.

"Quiet down now!" Aunt Wendy bellowed.

The girl slowly turned her head toward the front. Her gaze landed on him and her smile faded. He wanted to tell her he hadn't been spying on purpose, but wouldn't that just make things weirder? If he said it in front of all these people, it definitely would. Talk about a great first impression.

"Our director is going through some personal issues and has had to step down," his aunt said. She'd filled Sawyer in on the "personal issues" first thing that morning. Apparently her husband had been using the time she was spending in the theater to have sex with a coworker. Add that to the list of reasons why Sawyer wasn't interested in marriage.

The people onstage erupted in questions and comments all at once, so many it was hard to tell what anyone was saying.

Aunt Wendy swung her arms wide. "Calm down, everyone. I know how hard you've all worked these past two months, and we're not canceling. We've got a replacement director. He's from New York, and he's worked on a real movie and everything!"

That made him sound cooler than he was. He wrote a movie that got made into an indie film. The reviews were mostly good, though, and it had opened up opportunities he'd been dreaming about for years.

"So without further ado, I present your new director: Sawyer Raines." Aunt Wendy raised her eyebrows at him as though she expected a grand gesture. "You've got to say something," she whispered.

Sawyer looked at the actress in the middle of the stage again. She had her arms crossed and her jaw set. The girl was probably some kind of diva, the kind who thought the show should revolve around her. Well, he'd learned his lesson about actresses. Stay far away. For about the hundredth time, he wished he'd just said no. Drugs. Theater. Actresses. The slogan was the same—just say no.

He stepped forward and tried to force a smile. "I'm, uh, real happy to be here."

The dark-haired actress actually rolled her eyes. The rest were staring as if their lives depended on him. "So why don't you, uh, take it from where you left off last, I guess?"

Everyone except the actress with the attitude and the guy she'd been laughing with left the stage. The guy was at least two or three inches shorter than she was, though his puffy blond curls were trying to make up the difference.

Aunt Wendy slapped a playbook into Sawyer's hand.

"Why can't you direct again?" he asked.

"Because I do costumes and makeup. I can help you now, while you're getting the hang of things, but these next few weeks, I'll be far too busy." The two people onstage started up with their lines, their words echoing across the stage and through the empty auditorium. While the guy's voice was on the nasally side, the girl had a nice voice, though she needed to put some volume into it. She kept glancing at him and then whipping her head back to her acting partner.

"Miss Prism says that all good looks are a snare." She glanced at him again.

Is she aiming that line at me?

"They are a snare that every sensible man would like to be caught in," her acting partner replied. There was a time Sawyer would've agreed with that sentiment. But not anymore.

When she didn't say anything back, the guy nudged her. "Crap," she muttered.

"That's not even close to your line," the guy said with a laugh.

The girl looked at him again, those big doll eyes even wider. Then she turned back to the guy and said, "Crap," even louder. "What's my line?"

"I've barely got mine down," he said, then they both turned to Sawyer.

Aunt Wendy nudged him. "This is where you'd feed her the line."

Sure...if he'd been paying attention. He lifted the playbook, but it was upside down. Before he could get it turned upright and find where in the hell they were, she was off and talking again, but he could hear the frustration in her words. "...don't think I would care to catch a sensible man. I shouldn't know what to talk to him about."

Other people came onto the stage, delivering their lines—a Miss Prism and Dr. Chasuble—making large arm gestures.

Sawyer twisted in his squeaky seat to face his aunt. "So of course my mom says she's fine, but how's she really doing?

You think she's actually ready to let go of the house? It was supposed to be her and Dad's dream home."

Wendy raised her eyebrows and looked down her nose at him. "It's not doing her any good just sitting there, getting more rundown." Aunt Wendy was Dad's older sister, and while words couldn't express how much he appreciated the way she'd helped Mom in the six years since Dad passed away, he still worried. Surely with all the groups Mom belonged to, like book club, bridge—he was pretty sure there was a knitting one in there somewhere—she wouldn't get too lonely. But of course her life would never be the same. Activities couldn't replace someone you loved.

Sawyer blinked and swallowed past the lump rising in his throat. Even after all these years, it still got to him.

"Did you want us to start the next scene?" Distantly Sawyer realized whoever was asking the question was addressing him. "Or should we run through that one again?"

"You." He pointed at the dark-haired actress who'd asked the question. "What's your name?"

The girl crossed her arms. "Brynn?"

She was staring at him like that should mean something, and she'd made her name sound more like a question. Was she some actress from New York or LA? Maybe she was famous around here. "Okay, well, why don't you and…"

"My name's Leo, but I'm playing the role of Algernon," the dude announced. "So please refer to me as that as long as the production is running. I like to stay in character."

Sawyer wasn't even touching that. "Okay, why don't you guys take it from the top? I couldn't even hear your lines, Brynn. If you mumble, the audience will never know what you're saying."

Brynn shook her head, and he was pretty sure she said, "Seriously?" in that condescending way people did when it really meant, *You're a moron.*

So much for thinking he'd have to be careful about being attracted to her—he wouldn't cross that line for personal and professional reasons, but she obviously didn't consider him important enough to treat with respect, despite his new director position.

He glanced at Aunt Wendy, who hopped up and headed backstage, as if she knew he was fighting the desire to quit. He just had to get through…however long rehearsals lasted. Sawyer looked past the Brynn girl and the other actor to the props. They could use some serious work. Earlier today, he'd dug out Dad's old tools and bought everything else he'd need to get started on the lake house. He supposed he might as well bring in his tools and fix up this place, too. At least then he'd feel like he was contributing something toward making the production better.

And maybe in time, the cute girl standing onstage, throwing her arms around as she delivered her lines—though she was still too quiet—wouldn't look at him like she hated him.

Chapter Two

"Ugh, I just hate him," Brynn said as she entered the safety of the 1970s two-bedroom house she rented. She tried to slam the door to punctuate her statement, but it banged against the frame and bounced back at her, the knob slamming into her side. Stupid thing didn't line up right. She lifted the doorknob, pushed the heavy wood into place with the help of a solid hip bump, and finally managed to get the deadbolt to engage. Once the house was secure, she was ready to get back to the business of mentally tearing apart Sawyer Raines, the way she'd done the entire drive home.

Normally she reserved hate for things like olives and mushrooms and any other food with textures that weren't quite right. But Sawyer was one of the few people who deserved it. He'd sat there in the front, looking annoyingly hot and acting all superior—obviously he thought he was above directing their little play. When he'd said her name she'd waited for the recognition, but it never came. He didn't even know who she was. Part of her was glad, and part of her felt as invisible as she had back in high school.

Why'd he have to come and ruin her one escape from long boring days of talking to fake fish and the men who were obsessed with catching real ones?

And why would he return here after all these years? He obviously thought he was a famous screenwriter now, so why didn't he just stay in New York, where she wouldn't have to see his stupid face? Did he want to come be a big fish in a little pond instead of a guppy in a shark tank? She wanted to know, while simultaneously telling herself she didn't care.

Her two parakeets chirped at her as she neared them. "Hey, Lance. Gwen. How's Camelot these days? Probably more cagey than you thought it'd be, huh?" She fed them, watching as Lancelot went right for the food and Guinevere hopped on the swing as if she wanted to show off. It was harder to convince herself she wasn't still an awkward nerd when she was talking to her birds. Birds named for one of her favorite couples—hey, if they couldn't be together in the stories, at least they could be together in her living room in feathered form, right?

So, she wasn't your typical girl. But she wasn't the girl she used to be, either.

The bookshelf in the corner seemed to be calling to her. At one point she'd seriously considered burning all photographic evidence of high school, but there were her photo albums and her yearbook, hidden between her classic literature and romance novels. Some compulsion drew her toward them, like the spindle on the wheel of death in *Sleeping Beauty*. She knew she shouldn't reach for it, but here she was, doing it anyway.

She told herself she could face it, because she was now confident and coordinated and all the things she hadn't been until after high school.

Of *course* she tripped on the rug covering the mystery stain on the way over and had to brace herself on the bookshelf. So maybe she was still working on the coordination thing. She had to shift around her collection of ceramic kissing figurines to get out the albums. Then she carried them over to the couch, took a deep breath, and opened one.

It was even worse than she remembered. Wow, she'd made some bad choices, looks-wise. Like, hey, you know what would make my boring mousy-brown hair better? A perm. This pic was also from that disastrous year when she decided she should wear period clothing, like she was preparing for a Renaissance festival every day. Definitely not a wise decision if you're looking to fit in.

In her mind, she could still see the mocking faces, hear the whispers that included words like *nerd* and *weirdo*, and feel the residual heart-sinking sensation of how it felt to walk into a room and have all conversation stop. She remembered so many days walking down the halls of high school by herself, wishing she could be someone else.

Then there was the incident that shan't be named, the one she liked to pretend had only been a bad dream.

All the old wounds she'd thought had healed reopened, leaving her chest achy and raw.

Despite the pain, she opened her high school yearbook, junior year. She flipped to the page she'd obsessed over *way* too many times. Sawyer Raines stood by the sidelines in his football uniform, hair messy from the helmet he held in his hand, a red marker heart drawn around his face. Brynn had sat through every game, despite the stares and snide comments she'd gotten, all for the chance to see *him*.

She ripped out the page, crumpled it, and tossed it to the floor.

Her heart was beating way too fast, like a panic attack was coming on horseback to find her. Once again, she told herself that she was a different person now—that she didn't even look the same.

Her second year of college, Brynn roomed with a cosmetology student who always wanted to try out new hair treatments and styles. Or maybe it'd been her nice way of saying *you really need a makeover*. Laura had dyed Brynn's hair black, took scissors to it, and gave her a side-swept bang and fringe around the face. That day Brynn had looked into the mirror, noticed the contrast of her pale skin and the dark hair, the way it complemented what some people had called fish eyes, and thought, *This fits me*. She started leaning toward a mix of current and vintage styles with her clothing and accessories, finding a way to be herself yet fit into the modern world.

It had taken almost four years to undo the damage high school had done. And in one afternoon, she'd let the cocky jerk who had ruined her plans for one perfect, fairy-tale night all those years ago, unravel her confidence.

"I'm not going to let him do this to me," she muttered. She knew she was too sensitive about high school and always would be. But she was an actress, dammit! She could act like it didn't get to her, and hopefully, in time, it wouldn't. Tomorrow she would be confident yet mysterious. Strong and unimpressed by his looks or his accomplishments. In fact, she'd just ignore him.

And with any luck, he'd never recognize her.

• • •

Sawyer opened the screen door and dropped his laptop bag just inside. He'd spent several hours in the Daily Grind Coffeehouse writing and had lost track of how many cups of coffee he'd had. His footsteps echoed across the hardwood floor as he wandered into the living room.

This place had been rundown and in foreclosure when Dad bought it. The plan was to fix it up and make it the family's dream home—his parents had talked about the lake house as though everything would magically be perfect in their lives once they could move in. Sawyer had worked with Dad as he sketched out plans and made a list of all the cool things they could do with the space. Dad had even started a couple of projects, but his paying jobs always took precedence. Then he got sick. A few tests and the diagnosis was grim—ALS. So his muscles would only atrophy more.

He got weaker and weaker, until he couldn't work, and then eventually stopped being able to walk from room to room without help. Meanwhile, this house just got more covered with dust, its pretty view of the lake going to waste on the rats that'd built homes inside.

Not anymore, though.

Sawyer had called in an exterminator, and now he was going to turn this place into the home Dad had always dreamed it'd be—he only wished he'd done it sooner. Back in high school he'd been worried about sports and girls and trying to hide the fact that his dad could hardly move, like that was something he should be ashamed of. He'd put on a good enough act—everyone thought he'd had it all. He had lots of friends, a pretty girlfriend, and was the halfback on the championship-winning football team. Now he regretted not spending more time at home. He couldn't change the past, though, no matter how badly he wished he could.

He set down his bottle of water and picked up the sledgehammer. He'd planned on waiting until tomorrow morning, but he remembered the neighbors on both sides were all but deaf, and he needed something to do.

He decided to start in the living room. He was going to open it up and turn it into more of an entertainment area with easier access to the kitchen, the way he and Dad had talked about all those years ago. As he worked, bits of plaster sprayed his arms. Thinking of Mom, he dug out the goggles she'd gotten him because she was worried he'd hurt himself remodeling. The longer he thought about the new layout, the more excited he got over how it'd turn out. It might actually be hard to go back to his cramped Brooklyn studio after all this open space. And then there was still the possibility of moving to LA—from what he'd heard, it was about as pricey as New York, with more driving and less foot traffic, which he wasn't sure he'd like. Either way, though, it didn't take a whole lot of room to type, and right now he was starting to think he'd live alone forever, because it was just easier that way.

He was really getting into the rhythm, his muscles burning from exertion, when he heard a knock at the door. He lowered the hammer and wiped the sweat off his brow with his forearm.

"Don't you think it's kind of a bad time to be doing... whatever it is you're doing?" a female voice asked through the screen. "Some of us are trying to sleep."

He stepped into view of the door and stared at the dark-haired woman from the play. Brynn, he suddenly remembered.

Her jaw dropped. "You."

He smiled. "You."

"Great, just great." She started down the porch steps, heading away from the house.

"Wait. I'm sorry. I didn't mean to mess up your beauty sleep."

She spun around. Her dark hair was mussed and she had one of those eye-things that blocked out light while you slept on the top of her head like a headband.

"I didn't expect to see you around here," he said. "I thought you were some spoiled city chick."

"Yep, that's me. And now that I'm living here in the boonies, where people apparently remodel their houses during the middle of the night, I want to go back."

"Let me guess? LA?"

Brynn scowled at him.

Yep, he'd guessed right. The self-entitled air the LA type gave off was one of the reasons he was still dragging his feet about moving there, even though his agent insisted it'd be better for his career.

But then he noticed her pajama pants had monkeys on them, and he thought maybe she was different. She was here in North Carolina after all, and he figured people who took themselves too seriously didn't usually go around in monkey sleepwear. "So you live in this neighborhood, too?"

Her head dropped back, a gesture that seemed to say she couldn't believe she still had to talk to him. It should make him turn right back around and go inside, but he couldn't help himself. There was something about her that made him want to know more.

"I live right"—she swung her arm to the right, toward the little yellow house that an older lady named Ruth used to live in—"there. And yes, I can hear hammering at night. I didn't think anyone lived here. It's turned into one of those houses, like in movies, that kids dare each other to go inside."

Sawyer leaned against the doorframe. "Come on, it's not that bad. And I'm trying to make it better, but apparently I'm doing it too loudly." He shouldn't provoke her—they were going to be forced together most every day thanks to the play, and they'd need at least a semblance of a working relationship.

She pinched the bridge of her nose. "It's almost eleven."

He walked down the porch steps and she backed away from him as if he were going to attack her. He held up his hands. "I'm sorry, okay? I'll be working on it over the next few weeks, but I'll keep it to more polite hours."

"Good," she said, then bobbed her head, her hair flopping

in her face. She spun around on her heel and charged into the little house next door that looked like it could use plenty of renovations itself.

Sawyer felt himself smiling, the kind of wide smile he hadn't used in a while. He wasn't sure why it amused him that she hated him so much, but suddenly he found himself looking forward to tomorrow's rehearsal.

Chapter Three

Brynn's plan to ignore Sawyer had hit a snag that first night—how was she supposed to know *he* was the one banging around in the house next door? She wasn't sure what had possessed her to go yell about it instead of calling the police. Probably the fact that she'd been half asleep.

But other than that, she'd hardly spoken to him for the rest of the week. She even managed to focus and deliver her lines like she usually did—all out, not worrying about the too-cool-for-school guy in the front. He'd been on his computer most of the time, anyway. Not that she'd been paying attention. The guy wasn't taking hints very well, though—for some reason he kept trying to talk to her after rehearsal. Every time he tried, she darted away, afraid if she had a real conversation with him, he'd recognize her. Then she'd have to relive awful memories as he laughed at her, the nerdy girl who'd dared to go after someone like him.

Maybe he'd already figured it out. Surely he would've said something, though, right? Brynn's heart kicked up a few notches. Maybe that was why he wanted to talk to her.

In that case, she'd avoid him forever.

She peeked around the empty theater, satisfied everyone had left, and then got out the paints so she could work on the sets. Paul and his band were playing at the Tavern later tonight, so she had a few hours to kill before she headed over there. Since she used to work on sets when she was in drama club, she'd told Nora, the old director, that she'd spruce them up—and man did they need it.

Brynn made sure the ladder was steady, balanced the paints on the tray near the top, and then climbed up. Everyone else had been in a hurry to leave, since it was Friday night, and while the effect of the empty theater was a bit spooky, there was also something peaceful about it, like the magic was still hanging in the air, waiting for someone to grab hold of it and transform props and costumes into a story.

Humming a tune, she swirled the paintbrush in the yellow and stretched onto her toes to touch up the dingy-looking sun. She thought she heard the echo of a door and froze, brush hovering in the air. Keeping one hand clamped onto the ladder, she glanced behind her.

"Hello? Anyone there?" Her voice echoed across the stage and came back to her. She squinted into the darkness for a moment, then went back to humming and painting. The scent of the paint brought back memories from high school, when she used to watch the people onstage, wishing she could be performing, too. And now she was, a lead in one of her favorite plays.

With that happy thought, the humming morphed into singing "Honey, Honey" from *Mama Mia* at the top of her lungs—it'd been on her iPod earlier when she was driving, and really there was no way to sing it except all out.

"Brynn?"

She whipped around so fast her foot slipped. The paintbrush hit her in the chest, and the ladder screeched as she struggled to hold onto it. Hands came up on the sides of her waist to steady her, and then she was slowly lowered to the ground. When she turned around, she was chest to chest with Sawyer.

His eyes really are like emeralds.

She quickly shook that thought off. It was stupid and not in keeping with the ignoring-him plan. She stepped back, but of course the ladder was there. It knocked into the fake wall and the paint tipped over, splashing yellow splotches on the way down.

"Damn it!" She dropped to her knees to scoop the can up before it could make an even bigger mess. "What's wrong with you?" she said in Sawyer's direction. She wasn't a klutz anymore—this wasn't her fault, it was *his*. "You can't sneak up on someone like that."

He crouched down next to her. "I wasn't *trying* to scare you. And you're welcome for my catching you, by the way."

"I wouldn't have fallen if you weren't creeping around in the shadows."

He laughed and she shot him a dirty look. "I'm sorry, okay? I wasn't 'creeping around in the shadows.' I brought in my toolbox so I could work on the sets." He gestured toward a big gray box. "And I said your name so you'd know I was there, because I could tell from the way you were singing, you thought you were alone."

She lowered her chin, focusing on the paint. Was there some kind of rule that said she had to embarrass herself around him?

"You've got a great voice," he said. "Do you do musicals, too?"

She swiped her hair behind her ear. "I've done a couple, but they make me nervous. If you deliver a line wrong, you can usually cover pretty quickly. But you mess up in the middle of a song, then you're struggling to hit the right notes, and… Well, it's a lot harder for me to focus on the singing and acting all at once."

The way his mouth kicked into a half smile as he looked at her made her heart rate hitch up a few notches.

He reached out and then his fingers were in her hair and all she could do was freeze in place, her heart pounding so hard she was sure he could hear it. "You got a little paint in it." He brought his hand down and wiped it on his jeans.

"Oh. Thanks." Seconds stretched out between them and he was still staring at her. A flutter started low in her stomach, working its way up.

Stop it, Brynn. Stop it right now. She wasn't doing this again. She had to shut it down. No thinking about how she always thought he had artist's hands, though they weren't bad at catching a football, either. And definitely no thinking about the way his dark lashes lined his eyes and made the green stand out even more.

"I better get a rag and clean this up before it sets." She grabbed a spare rag, hurried to the bathroom to wet it, and then rushed back.

Sawyer had a mop out—she had no idea where he found it—and was wiping up the last of the paint. The floor cleaned up easily enough, which just left the yellow splashed across the blue sky to take care of.

"See, no harm done." Sawyer's gaze lowered to her shirt, which had a dashed yellow pattern thanks to the paintbrush rolling down it. His shirt had a smear from when she'd been pressed up against him.

She wiped at her shirt, though the paint was already dry. "I'm wearing my painting clothes, so it's not a big deal."

He gave her another half smile. "Dang, I thought I was going to get to see you change again."

Her face flooded with heat. "I… That was…"

He reached out and squeezed her shoulder. "I'm kidding."

The other half of his mouth got in on the smile, and it made those supposedly dormant butterflies come back full-force.

Was he actually flirting with her? She took a couple steps back, not sure how to handle him. "I better try to fix the sky."

"While you're working on that, I'm going to see if I can't repair the sagging walls of the house." Sawyer opened up his toolbox and took out a hammer and a box of nails. "You can keep singing if you want. Don't hold back on my account."

Brynn picked up her paintbrush and started for the ladder. "No thanks, but if *you* want to sing, feel free."

"I think you'd change your mind if you heard me sing."

She smiled at him, and he smiled back. Then she realized she was blinking way too quickly—her body's automatic attempt to flirt. Because nothing says *Hey, look how hot I am* like rapid-style blinking. She quickly turned to the work in front of her, not wanting to encourage him. It was possible, though, that he wasn't *quite* as awful as she'd thought he was. Maybe he'd changed since high school—she certainly had.

A few minutes later, Brynn bit her lip and studied the sky. It was looking more green than blue. Perhaps it'd be better to let it dry and then attempt to paint a white cloud over the top.

When she dropped down off the ladder, she peeked at Sawyer. He was putting nails into the walls of the house backdrop, the muscles in his arm and back moving with each swing of the hammer. His tongue was poking out between his lips and his forehead was creased in concentration. It was no wonder she'd chosen him to obsess over in high school. Even now that she wasn't all sappy in love with him, he was still one of the best-looking guys she'd ever seen.

"Can you come hold this up for me?" he asked. "I can't quite keep it in place and really swing like I need to."

Crap. He must've known she was staring. She moved closer and stretched onto her toes to hold the canvas in place. His body brushed hers as he set a nail, and her breath came out shaky. She caught a whiff of his cologne—musky, with a hint of something that smelled like freshly cut grass.

If she wasn't going to think about him like *that*, then she needed to look away. And cover her nose. She tried to swallow but her throat was too dry. Water. She desperately needed water.

"Do you mind?" He was so close, she could feel the vibrations of his deep voice.

Oh, holy crap, could he tell I was sniffing him? I'm never going to be able to come to rehearsal again.

He lifted his hand higher, extending the nails to her. She took them and tried to focus on not dropping them.

He finished driving in one nail and then held out his hand for another. "So why'd you leave LA?"

"What?" she asked, trying to follow the question. If only she hadn't been so distracted by the muscles and the closeness.

Sawyer lowered the hammer and looked at her. That's when she remembered that the other night he'd said something about her being from LA. She'd been too angry at seeing him again—at finding out he'd apparently moved in next door—to tell him he'd guessed wrong.

"I'm surprised you'd come here when there are so many acting opportunities there," he said.

She was going to correct him, but then she'd have to explain that she was from here, and then he'd probably ask what part, and what if he realized who she was? After their conversation about her changing her shirt, it would only add to the humiliation, and then she really *would* have to pull out of the play. Besides, being an actress from California sounded way cooler and more exciting than her real life. Plus, it'd throw him off if he ever did start to think he knew her from somewhere. So she decided to just go with it.

"I needed a break from all the pressure of LA." Wasn't

that what people said? Sounded okay enough. "I ran away from it all, only to end up back at the theater." She smiled, liking her made-up past. A bit tragic, but like she couldn't help but be drawn to the stage. Which was kind of true.

"Yeah, I needed to get away for a while, too. Not from theater, but from everything in New York. Things got messy there and... Anyway, taking a break was the right move. Plus, my mom needed me here."

Aww, he came to help his mom. As much as she wanted to keep on hating him, he wasn't making it easy. She supposed saying something nice to him wouldn't *kill* her. And most Hollywood actresses would probably be impressed by him. So really, she was simply playing a role, not forgiving him for hurting her in the past. "Well, it's very impressive that you made a movie."

"My aunt made me sound more important than I am. I'm just a screenwriter. I write movies."

"I actually do know what a screenwriter is." There he went, being condescending again.

"Right, of course." He drove in the nail that was sticking halfway out and then reached for another one. "You know, it's funny, I'm actually digging this play, and all that goes into it."

Damn, now he was being nice again. She couldn't help but return the smile he flashed her. They were having a decent conversation, and she hadn't made a total fool of herself in the past few minutes, which was always a bonus. "Oh yeah?"

"Yeah. I never would've guessed it. Back at my high school, the only people who did the theater stuff were huge dorks."

All her happy vibes died, anger rising up in their place. She slammed the remaining nails on the fake flower bush next to him and strode back to her art supplies, gathering them up as fast as possible. Painting the rest would have to wait.

"Brynn?" Sawyer swung his arms out, the hammer still in his hand. "Where are you going?"

"I've got other things to do."

"Wait," he said, but she didn't. What a *jerk*! There she'd been, thinking she was wrong, that maybe he'd changed, but *nooo*, he was the same arrogant ass he'd been in high school.

And this dork was going back to staying far, far away from him.

• • •

He so didn't get women. One second he'd thought maybe he and Brynn could actually get along—in fact, he'd been starting to have thoughts about her that pushed the boundaries of professionalism. The next, she was storming off as if he'd offended her. Sawyer went back over the conversation in his head, but nothing stuck out.

He shouldn't be thinking about her anyway. Not how cute she was when she was onstage, putting everything she had into her acting. Not her voice. Or the scent of her floral shampoo or perfume. And definitely not the way she'd felt in his arms, as brief as it had been. That was why he'd asked her to help him, even though he was perfectly capable of holding up the canvas and putting the nails in at the same time.

The last actress he'd dated had been like one of those pain scale ratings they showed you in the hospital. One minute Zoey would be all happy with a big smile on her face, then she'd be weepy, and then she'd be fine. He never knew what would set her off, but she was smart and pretty and driven, and best of all, interested more in her career than their relationship. They'd both agreed on a casual arrangement, that their work should come first, which was perfect.

But then she'd gotten her big break—a role on a TV show. And suddenly she wanted him to visit the set all the time and start looking at lofts so they could move in together. When he told her he might be moving to LA, she'd asked if she was even a consideration in his plans. He hadn't immediately answered, because she hadn't been, though he knew better than to say that to her. Then she'd started throwing things at his head, telling him how she'd cheered him on while he'd been writing his screenplay, and how could he do this to her?

That would've been bad enough, but she had to take it a step further, manipulating him in a way that still made his blood boil whenever he thought about it. He'd vowed no more actresses then, and he couldn't believe he'd let himself think that it could be different with a girl here, just because he was in North Carolina and this was a small production. Brynn was obviously a Hollywood actress at heart, like all the rest of them. Probably a liar, too, and even if she wasn't, she definitely had the moody thing down pat.

She'd gone from angry to smiling, then back to angry.

But when she was smiling… He closed his eyes, picturing how her smile brought out her cheeks, how it lit up her entire face in an innocent yet sexy way.

Sawyer opened his eyes and shook his head. Say she wasn't a crazy moody person—what was he going to do? Considering his position as director, he shouldn't so much as flirt with her, and definitely nothing further than that could happen. In fact, he should probably stay away from all conversation outside the play.

It'd be a lot easier if he weren't so curious about the girl. Or if he hadn't spent the last week watching her, wondering why her face lit up onstage, backstage—whenever anyone but him talked to her. Maybe she thought he didn't take this job seriously. He could try to think of something to show her he did—his name was attached, too, and he found he really did want the play to be good. But what he should probably do was just forget about it. He wasn't going to be here long enough to make friends, and that was how he wanted it. In and out, clean and simple.

He finished working on the sets, wiggling them to see if they'd stand up to being moved around, then gathered his tools and headed to Mom's, doing his best to put the female species out of his mind entirely.

But when he stepped inside Mom's place, he found not just Mom, but also a blond girl who seemed vaguely familiar. Mom was hugging him before he got a good look, though. "There you are! I was starting to think you weren't going to come home again." She turned toward the girl. "He's been working on that remodeling project I was telling you about."

And that was when it hit him. She was a daughter of one of Mom's friends, the one she used to always want him to date growing up.

Oh, hell. I'm being set up. Sawyer glanced at the door, though he knew it was far too late to run, then attempted a polite smile. "Kayla Norman. It's good to see you again."

"I wasn't sure you'd remember me," she said with a grin that showed off the fact that the braces had worked.

"Of course I do." While she was cute, he'd never gone for her. Partly because Mom wanted him to date her, but mostly because he'd been dating Carly Johnson at the time—Mom never liked his girlfriend, so she pretended he was single instead of acknowledging her. In the end, Carly dumped him in front of the entire school, so apparently Mom's instincts were right.

But that didn't mean he was going to let her set him up now.

Mom patted his arm, trying to subtly pull him closer to the blonde. "Kayla's in my book club, and now that you're in town, I thought, wouldn't it be fun to all have dinner? I better check on it. You two go ahead and catch up." She ducked into the kitchen in record speed.

He stared at the archway for a moment, then turned toward Kayla. *Well, I'm stuck now, so I guess I might as well be nice.* He sat next to Kayla on the couch. She was still cute, short and blond. Actually, she was even prettier than he remembered, with high cheekbones and full lips.

"Wow, you look the same," she said. "Just like you did the day you made all those touchdowns in the championship game."

Sawyer didn't really know how to respond to that. It wasn't like that many years had passed, so of course he looked the same. Probably not like he was going to run across a football field any minute, though. "So...you're in my mom's book club."

"Yeah." She smiled wider.

He was about to lean in and whisper a joke about how he thought this was a misguided set-up, but then he noticed the tilt of her head and the way she was staring at him. He wasn't sure she was in on the set-up, but she definitely was interested.

I wish Brynn would look at me like that. His eyebrows drew together. Where had that come from? He barely knew the girl. Didn't know anything about her except she was an actress. With a pretty voice. Who wore monkey pajamas.

"I was thinking that we could maybe go get a drink after dinner." Kayla pressed against him and licked her lips. Wow, she was trying hard.

"It shouldn't be taking my mom this long. I better just go check that she's okay." Sawyer strode into the kitchen. Mom was leaning against the counter, reading a book as if she didn't have company at all.

She glanced up as he got closer. "What are you doing? Go talk to Kayla."

"Mom." He attempted a smile, but it felt more like a grimace. "I need you to not try to set me up. I'm only going to be in town for a little while and—"

"But what if you meet the perfect girl? Then you'd consider staying, right?"

"Sorry, Ma. I'm lucky that I can travel right now, and the truth is, I'll probably go back to New York, pack up, and move to LA." He was thinking he might as well take the chance, though the thought made him miss New York already. Knowing Mom would sense weakness if he didn't act excited, he pushed on. "I can get in better there with the people who've shown interest in the screenplay I'm writing. Face-to-face meetings go a long way."

Mom's shoulders sagged. "I just want you to find a nice girl and settle down. By the time your father and I were your age, we already had you. And if we hadn't gotten started that young, then…" She glanced out the kitchen window and everything inside him started to crack. She tried not to say anything, but he knew she was worried he'd have the same health issues as Dad. In a lot of ways, it was why he'd be hesitant to ever fully commit to someone in the picket-house, have-two-point-three-kids way. He didn't want someone he loved to have to take care of him like that, even though the doctors all said it was unlikely.

Mom turned back to him, eyes shiny with tears, and the crack inside him widened to a gaping hole. "I want you to be happy."

"I am happy."

She clicked her tongue. "You are not. I've heard it in your voice for months, then I see you, and you've got too much stress in your life. You need a break."

"That's why I'm here." Honestly, he couldn't remember the last time he'd been truly happy—probably when he sold his script. Even the movie premiere was tainted with bad memories, thanks to his ex. This past week when he was working on the lake house was actually the best he'd felt in a long time. And there for a few minutes today with Brynn, but he was trying not to think about that. "Maybe once I make a name for myself I can visit more. Or maybe you could move to California, too. It'd be sunny and—"

"I'd never leave North Carolina. This is where I belong." *This is where all my memories are*, she didn't say, but she wrapped her hand around the locket on her neck. Dad had given her the necklace for their first wedding anniversary, and Sawyer knew it now held a picture of her two boys—him and Dad.

When Dad passed away after several months of barely living, Sawyer had wondered if Mom would be relieved she didn't have to pour every ounce of energy into taking care of his needs anymore. He hated himself for even thinking it now, especially after seeing how destroyed she'd been. He knew she would've taken care of him forever if it meant not losing him.

Mom dropped her hand and opened the oven door. The scent of roasted bass filled the air. He hadn't thought he was that hungry, but he'd suffer through anything—even an awkward blind date with his mom watching—if it meant eating her specialty dish.

Mom walked to the doorway of the kitchen. "Kayla sweetie, we're just grabbing the food. Go ahead and have a seat at the table and we'll be right there." She glanced over her shoulder at Sawyer. "Can you grab the plates?" Sawyer stacked three plates and placed the silverware on top of them.

As they were about to step into the dining room, Mom leaned in close and whispered, "And just give Kayla a chance. Please? For me? I really think you'll like her."

So much for thinking he'd gotten through to her. Unfortunately for his dating life, he was a sucker when it came to his mom.

Chapter Four

Brynn pushed into the Tavern. She'd killed a few hours in a restaurant, studying lines and marking up her playbook in the places she needed to work on. What kept coming into her head, though, was Sawyer's hands on her waist. That moment when everything had changed and it felt like something magical was hanging in the air between them. But he'd only been getting paint out of her hair.

She told herself to focus on the fact that he'd called her a dork, even if he didn't realize he had. Tomorrow she'd be sure to make a comment about how jocks were dumb. That'd show him. To err was human. To forgive a guy like Sawyer Raines, not worth her time.

Brynn sat across from Paul, who was scrubbing a hand over his face, his eyes redder than usual. "How'd the numbers look today?"

He let out a long exhale. "We're hanging in there. Still down a bit from last year, but it'll pick up. July and August are always big months for us."

Bigfish Bait and Tackle had been in their family for three

generations. When Mom and Dad retired last year, Paul had taken over and asked if she wanted to help him run it. She'd just gotten out of college and needed a job. Not to mention she'd grown up in that shop, running through the aisles and making necklaces and bracelets out of fishing lures—Dad used to tell her he'd sell them and she'd make them all rich. Paul had played in the aisles and helped out, too, and they both felt the pressure not to screw up their family's legacy.

"Maybe we should run coupons in the paper," Brynn said. "A buy-one-get-one-half-off special. See if it'll bring in more people."

Paul set his beer down and nodded. "We can try it out, see if it's profitable. You'll take care of getting it in the paper, right?"

"I'll talk to my contact there." Really, Mr. Daniels was everyone's contact for the paper, but it sounded fancier when she referred to him as hers. She had to find a way to make it more dramatic, right? Once in a while having a literature degree with a minor in theater seemed like a waste—she should've taken more business classes—but she'd enjoyed those years. And while she didn't have grand visions of becoming a Broadway or Hollywood actress the way she had back in high school, she certainly hadn't pictured herself helping run the Bait and Tackle forever.

"Sometimes I feel like we've turned into Mom and Dad. You're always going on and on about numbers, while I'm bent over the register, complaining about how we have to watch the same damn fishing show over and over."

Paul laughed, then frowned. "That's a bit depressing, come to think of it. Hopefully soon we'll both find significant others and have kids of our own running around and wreaking havoc on the merchandise like we did. And the World Fishing Network is always adding new shows to the mix."

"It doesn't much matter; they're all the same. Watching

another person fish is about as entertaining as watching grass grow. And as for marriage and kids, well, in case you haven't noticed, neither one of us is very close to that possibility." As soon as she said it, she wanted to take it back. Paul had thought he'd found the one about six months ago, and had even bought a ring, but then he discovered she was cheating on him. It still made Brynn's blood boil when she thought about it.

Paul leaned forward, propping his elbows on the table. She thought he was going to say something about his ex, but then he smiled and said, "Speak for yourself. I'm out every night working on making babies. The ladies love me, in case you haven't noticed."

"Ew." Brynn picked up the cardboard coaster and threw it at his head, but she couldn't help but laugh. If he really was that guy, she'd launch into a lecture about treating women with respect, but she knew deep down he wanted to find a nice girl and settle down.

Paul lifted his hand in a wave, and Brynn glanced back. Dani and Wes were heading their way. Brynn stood to greet them—she'd always been a hugger. It had taken a while for Dani to get used to it—she used to stiffen up—but now she actually leaned in for it as they exchanged greetings.

Instead of taking the two chairs, Wes pulled Dani onto his lap and wrapped his arms around her. They were in that kiss-every-five-seconds, newly engaged stage of love. Maybe it made her weird, but Brynn always got a bit of a love-high off people like that. Of course it triggered the longing to have someone special in her life, but it also meant that love like that still happened. So she could be patient. If a great guy could come along any day now, though, she definitely wouldn't complain.

"So," Wes said. "What's going on?"

"A whole lot of nothing," Paul said, then everyone turned

to her.

"Just work and then rehearsing the play," Brynn said. "I kind of want to strangle the new director, so there's that."

Dani nudged Brynn with her elbow, something Brynn was starting to get used to. "I thought you were Team Sunshine and Rainbows." When Dani had been talking favorite basketball teams with the guys last weekend, Brynn had said she was Team Sunshine and Rainbows. Seemed like a good team to root for.

"I'm still for all that. It's just this guy…" What to say about Sawyer? He was hot and frustrating, nice and insulting—all at the same time. Suddenly she was picturing him back in high school, when he was all those things as well, except for nice. "He's one of those guys who oozes cockiness."

"Ugh, I hate that type of guy." Dani grinned at Wes. "Not sure how I ended up engaged to one."

"You got lucky, that's how," Wes said, and then he and Dani started kissing. Paul rolled his eyes and Brynn shrugged and sat back in her chair, knowing it could be a while before the couple came up for air.

"There's Rob," Paul said, tapping the table in front of Wes and Dani. "We better go get set up."

He and Wes pushed away from the table. Dani stood, too. She glanced at Brynn and then turned to Wes and put her hand on his arm. "I think Brynn and I will just hang out here. We'll come up front when you start your set."

"Good luck getting past all the groupies," Wes joked. "Actually, *your* groupies will probably be here tonight. Five bucks they demand the sexy singer come onstage again."

"No telling them to ask me, or the bet's off."

They exchanged another quick kiss, and then Wes, Paul, and Rob headed toward the tiny room in the back so they could set up. Dani flagged down a waitress, asked for a beer, and turned to Brynn. "Whatcha want?"

"I'll just have a Coke." What she really wanted was one of those fruity lemonades, but the only time she'd tried to order it here, the waitress looked at her like she was asking for a kidney.

Once they were alone again, Dani propped her elbow on the table. "Sorry, you were saying something about the director of your play driving you crazy?"

"I knew him in high school," Brynn said, the admission taking some of the pressure off her chest but knotting her stomach at the same time. "His name's Sawyer Raines, and he was one of the popular guys. And I was at the opposite end of the cool crowd. High school was a super awkward time for me."

To Dani's credit, she didn't act like that was a given or even try to mock surprise. Brynn powered on. "I mean, I'm still not like most girls, I know that. I work in a fishing shop, yet I like theater and show tunes—if my life were one big Broadway musical, I'd be psyched. I ramble too much and I'm not what anyone would call smooth. And I've come to peace with all that. Or at least I thought I did. But seeing him, it brought back those bad memories, and I keep telling myself not to let him get to me, but he makes me feel so self-conscious. And then suddenly I'm tripping and dropping paint on my clothes and..." *Thinking about what it would be like to kiss him, the same way I used to back in high school.* "I hate feeling like this again."

"I think we all have those people who bring out our insecurities," Dani said. "But just so you know, I like who you are."

"Maybe now. You thought I was weird at first—admit it."

Dani laughed. "I did not think you were weird. I've just never met someone quite so bubbly and excited about hugs, and I wasn't sure how to take it. I'm used to hanging out with guys. But I'm glad we met, and I'm totally down with the hugging thing now. From you, anyway. Don't go spreading that around."

Brynn smiled, warmth filling her chest. "Thanks. I'm glad I met you, too." That was the truth. All of her close girlfriends had moved away, and she was happy to have someone to talk to. Their drinks showed up and for a moment they sat and sipped them, the garbled seventies hits from the jukebox floating through the air.

Brynn tipped back the last of the Coke, again wishing it were strawberry or raspberry lemonade. "I think I need to start actively looking for a guy, because Prince Charming sure ain't knocking at my door. Guess you don't know any cute single guys."

Dani twisted her cup, leaving circles on the wooden tabletop. "Sorry. The only single guys I know are Paul and the other pilot who works with Wes. He happens to also be in his fifties and bald."

"Hot," Brynn deadpanned. "Add an unhealthy love for fishing, and I'm sold."

Dani laughed. "Between working with Wes on marketing for his new helicopter tours and planning this wedding with his mom's help, I haven't met many other people. I did, however, land a part-time job at a basketball camp that runs over the summer. Maybe there will be a cute coach there. I'll keep a lookout."

"No jocks. They're cute, but I don't mesh with that type." Once more, Sawyer's face flashed through her mind. The current version. Ugh, she needed to get him out of her head and focus on finding a guy she actually had a shot with. Part of her problem was she always expected her dates to be these life-changing moments filled with air-crackling chemistry. She'd only had two steady boyfriends since high school, and neither one had given her that magical I-want-to-be-around-you-every-second sensation. Maybe it was her. Maybe she'd OD'd on fictional love stories and real guys couldn't compare—Paul constantly told her that she had unrealistic expectations. She supposed she could lower them a little bit.

Guess I just need to settle for a guy who doesn't make me want to vomit.

It was a low bar. Surely someone could reach it.

Over the course of the night, Brynn met a couple guys who fit her new standard. She managed to scare the first prospect away when she responded to him using a Shakespeare quote. In her defense, he was the one who commented that he was ready to stop watching the news because it was so depressing lately. All she'd said was, "Life's but a walking shadow, a poor player that struts and frets his hour upon the stage, and then is heard no more." *Macbeth.* What a buzz kill—she should've known better.

The other guy showed a lot of interest, which was flattering, but he kept massaging her back and the contact made her skin crawl. Bar lowered or not, that wasn't the way it was supposed to be. And hello, she'd just met him. What was wrong with holding hands? Or at least asking a couple get-to-know-you questions first?

So she ditched the guy as nicely as possible, made her way to the stage area, and pushed into the back room.

Dani glanced at her as she entered. "How'd it go?"

Brynn shook her head. "It didn't."

"You'll have better luck next time. Bars aren't really a good place to meet guys anyway."

"So where do I go, then? How do people even meet anymore?"

"Honestly, I have no idea. I tried Internet dating for a little while, and I met one decent guy, but I was already in love with Wes, so it didn't really take." Dani leaned against the wall and watched Wes as he put away his guitar.

"Well, I don't have a best friend who's a guy, so…"

Dani twisted to face her. "It wasn't just that we were friends, though. I mean, that was awesome, because we already knew each other so well, but I felt this shift. Every look, every touch—it was like…like my heart was trying to clue me in before my head got it." She swiped her bangs behind her ear and they immediately fell forward. "I guess I'm saying you'll know it when the time's right. It sort of hits you and makes you feel like you've been mowed down by a linebacker. But in a good way." Dani winced, ran her fingers over her forehead, then raised her voice. "You're turning me into a sappy girl, Wes Turner. I hope you're happy."

He shot her a grin over his shoulder. "Couldn't be happier."

If comparing love to being hit by a football player is sappy, I don't even want to know what Dani would think of my lines of poetry. Or the quotes I love from plays and books. What's beyond sappy?

Still, she wanted the sappy.

"I think I'm going to take off," Brynn said.

Dani actually initiated the hug this time. "Call me if you want to chat or go out or whatever. I'll even attempt to be a good wingman if you want to hit up a club or whatever."

"Thanks." Brynn told the guys good-bye and headed to her car. As she made the twenty-minute drive home, she mentally scolded herself for comparing every guy to Sawyer tonight, the same pathetic way she'd done in high school. But when he'd been the one mere inches from her, shrinking away hadn't been her first instinct. Ugh, maybe this was all karma. She'd turned down perfectly nice guys back then because they weren't the dream scenario she'd played out in her mind, the one where Sawyer realized she was the girl for him and dumped his cliché cheerleader girlfriend for her.

Billy Miller liked me. We were both in drama club, and I brushed him off. The guy used to be tall and scrawny, as awkward as she was if not more. But he'd filled out, bulked up, and now he constantly had a pretty girl on his arm. Brynn gripped her steering wheel tighter. It just proved that even nerds who turned hot let their looks go to their heads. Hotness equaled jerkiness.

When she pulled up to her house a few minutes later, she noticed the lights next door were on. The lawn still needed mowing and weeds were climbing up the porch railing and sides of the house—so far, she didn't see much of a change.

Brynn got out of her car and noticed a dark figure on the porch.

He walked closer, his footsteps heavy on the wooden planks. She knew it would be Sawyer, but when he stepped into the glow of the porch light, her breath still caught. It wasn't fair that the sight of him sent her pulse racing. For a moment, they simply regarded each other. She had no idea what to say after the way things had ended this afternoon.

Does he even know I was mad? Simply looking at him, she got angry all over again. She'd been considering letting go of the past—she wanted to. But then he'd gone and made her feel like the awkward girl she used to be.

Hotness equals jerkiness, hotness equals jerkiness—she planned on repeating it until she got it through her head.

"I'm just measuring out a few things," Sawyer said, breaking the silence. "Don't worry, I finished with the noisy stuff already."

She lifted her chin. "Good." Another beat of staring, then she started up the steps of her own porch.

"Brynn." There was something about the way he said her name that made the anger she was desperately trying to hold on to slip from her body. "You wanna run lines? We've got this *Romeo and Juliet* matchup going on, facing balconies—or porches or whatever."

Damn, how could she resist a *Romeo and Juliet* reference? Although, technically, Juliet was the only one on a balcony.

Hmm…what would an LA actress who wasn't hung up on him say? "Sorry, but I had such a crazy time at this bar tonight, dancing and drinking, and you know how that is. I'm completely exhausted." She sighed and added a hair flip for good measure. "Maybe some other time."

Before she broke character, she hurried into her house. It would've felt like such a smooth exit if the stupid door didn't refuse to close. She lifted it like she usually did, but even then, it only made this grinding screech. And then one of the hinges completely gave way. Her door banged against the frame and then fell off altogether, crashing down onto her porch with a loud *bang* that echoed for an eternity.

She stared at it, hoping that her vision would suddenly shift and the universe would be like, *Just kidding, I wouldn't do that to you.*

Sawyer strolled up the sidewalk, toolbox in hand. "Havin' some trouble, ma'am?" he asked with a big grin, playing up the southern accent. She hadn't realized he'd been holding it back until he let it out full-force. "Did that partyin' you mentioned include pumping steroids?"

She frowned at him. "The door's been messed up forever and I tried to close it and it—"

He stepped over the door, bringing him so close that all her words suddenly left her. "No worries. I'll take care of it." In addition to the cologne he'd been wearing earlier, there was a hint of sawdust mixed in now. He was dirt-smudged in a completely sexy way, as if it had been applied in all the right places. "That is, if you won't call the police on me for making noise this late."

She gave him a little shove and he grinned at her.

Hotness equals…he's really hot.

"If you'd be so kind as to set this inside." He handed her the toolbox—which was heavier than she expected and came dangerously close to slipping from her fingers and breaking her toe as she set it down—and then bent to grab the door. She couldn't help but notice he had a nice butt to go with his nice everything else. He lifted the door and leaned it against the side of the house. "I can't believe it's held on at all. These screws are too tiny for such a heavy door." He glanced at her with his eyebrows raised, as if waiting for a reply. Was he expecting her to comment on the tiny screws as well?

"I guess I was too busy trying to maneuver it into place to notice the screw size. Because, yeah. I usually pay attention to that."

His lips broke into the kind of smile that left a girl a little light-headed. "You're cute, you know that?" He reached out and squeezed her hand—such a simple gesture, but it certainly got her heart pounding. Then his fingers curled around her palm and her stomach started doing somersaults.

This was probably how he got all the girls. He was Sawyer Raines, the guy who'd dated only the prettiest and most popular in high school. The guy who'd walked *away* from her like he'd catch her nerdiness when she'd tried to talk to him back then.

She pulled her hand free and turned to the toolbox. "So what do you need?"

He stared at her for a moment, his steady green eyes boring into her. "The electronic screwdriver. It's right there on top."

Their fingers brushed when she handed it over, like they did in all her romance books and movies. Tingling heat wound up her arm. It was becoming harder and harder to hold on to all the things she'd told herself to remember on the drive here.

Especially when he got to work on her door. Hot guys working with tools instantly became that much hotter. The fact that he was helping her out showed that he wasn't a *complete* jerk—she wasn't ruling out partial jerk, though. In fact, thinking he was nice was what had gotten her in trouble in high school. She remembered how he'd once picked up the sweater she'd dropped. He'd held it out for her, and she'd stared, unable to form words.

Then there was the time her biology partner was being teased and Sawyer had told the other guys on the football team to leave him alone—that had been when she knew he was more than the typical popular jock, and her crush grew to borderline obsession.

Regardless of a nice gesture here and there, though, she was no longer stupid enough to think that Sawyer Raines would ever fall for her. Flirt, sure, maybe take her out a time or two. He probably even thought he could use her for a night. Well, he had another thing coming.

She wanted an actual nice guy, one who'd *always* been nice and who would appreciate her for who she was. She was done with dating guys for sport. It was like catch and release fishing, and she needed to hook one that she didn't want to throw back, one that wanted to be caught. A simple glance into the past would reveal that she and Sawyer weren't meant to be.

She had a flash of the day she'd decided to be bold and ask Sawyer out. She'd dressed up—purple bohemian skirt, black tank top, and nearly every necklace and bracelet she owned. She'd used curling mousse in her hair, accidentally swallowed Listerine—which burned quite a bit on the way down, FYI—and planned out the exact time she'd talk to him.

Brynn's pulse had picked up speed as Sawyer came around the corner, brown hair messy, one strap of his backpack casually draped over his shoulder. Perfect. Like always. And maybe he would be hers soon.

She had gulped a mouthful of air and stepped into his path. "Hey, Sawyer." Her hands were shaking and she gathered her skirt in them to try to hide it.

He'd looked down at her, his eyebrows drawn together.

"How's it going?" she asked, wondering if she should move past the small talk and blurt out what she wanted to ask him. This was the moment she'd pictured in her mind for a good year, after all. She needed to just go for it.

But then she had become acutely aware of the fact that drops of sweat were forming on her forehead and her heart felt like it might pop right out of her chest. "I, um. I was wondering if you'd want to…go to prom…with me?"

He stared at her like she'd spoken to him in another language, the lines on his forehead deepening. "Prom…?" He shook his head and walked away.

It was right then that she'd understood why people called it a crush. It was like she was a disgusting bug he'd stomped on, and all she could do was lie there, one leg twitching as the life slowly drained from her.

She'd leaned against the wall, feeling hot tears prick her eyes. Why had she thought he might say yes? What had possessed her to try? She'd cast one last glance at his retreating back, then called her mom, told her she was sick, and begged her to come pick her up.

Even now, Brynn could feel the residual pain in her chest. The Jane Austen–inspired dress she'd made for the prom she never got to go to was still in her closet, unworn thanks to the rejection she felt every time she looked at it. The accidental underwear flashing during the school play happened a couple weeks after, and then she had just counted the days until school was over, her goal becoming survival.

They should have a warning over the doors of high schools so people wouldn't be shocked at how awful it was.

Something like, *Abandon all hope, ye who enter here.*

"Could you help me move it into place?" Sawyer asked.

Brynn blinked, surprised at the tears there. She wasn't crying, but they were near the surface, seconds from dropping if she didn't choke them back. On autopilot, she grabbed the other side of the door and held it as Sawyer stood way too close, smelling way too good, putting the screws in place.

So he was being nice to her right now. Did that make it okay to have treated her so badly back when she was a bit of a disaster? Could she really just forget about the way he'd crushed her?

The hurt rose up again, the pinch in her chest saying the answer was no. What she needed to do was go back to cold indifference, no matter what.

She needed to get Sawyer Raines out of her mind for good.

• • •

Sawyer walked into his house—no, scratch that. Suddenly he was thinking of it as his, and he needed to remind himself that after it became the perfect house, he was going to sell it. He set down the toolbox, then glanced out the window facing Brynn's place. He couldn't figure out the girl.

He'd also slipped up, telling her she was cute, when that thought was supposed to stay *inside* his head. *Way to keep things professional, Raines.*

Not only was she an actress—the exact type of girl he'd sworn off thanks to his ex—but he was basically her boss right now. So it'd be totally unprofessional to start up something with that beautiful, sassy girl next door.

Yet…

Well, when she had been standing there staring at her fallen door, he'd wanted to comfort her. He'd found himself staring at her lips, thinking about what it would be like to kiss her. And when she pulled away, he wanted to be able to direct her to come closer instead.

Why was this girl messing with his head so much? He needed to shake it off, focus on his work. He hadn't written all day. He eyed his computer, but with how unsettled he felt right now, he'd probably end up filling the screen with a page of swearwords and exclamation points. Maybe have a zombie kill off a character or two, which would be weird, since it wasn't a zombie screenplay.

He needed another escape. A distraction to keep his mind busy.

Luckily, he remembered there was an old TV/DVD combo that Dad had left there ages ago. He'd stowed it here so that if the fish weren't biting or he needed a break from things at work or home, he'd sneak over to the empty house and kick back with a movie.

Sawyer carried the television out of the side closet and placed it on a box in the living room. The screen was tiny— especially when compared to the fifty-five-inch flat screen that he had back in New York. It happened to be the most valuable item he owned, and he wasn't sure if that was awesome or sad.

Sawyer stuck the plug for the TV into the outlet, hoping it'd work.

Not only did it work, but when he ejected the DVD it was *Die Hard*. Classic. He vaguely remembered Dad not being able to find it one day. In fact, he'd given up after they'd both spent a good hour looking for it, and sent Sawyer to go buy another copy.

Sawyer pulled out the sleeping bag from the room he was crashing in. Paired with an air mattress, it was actually pretty comfortable. Mom wanted him to go back and sleep at her place every night, and he would from time to time, but something about waking up to see the sun rising over the lake made him ready to work on the house. If he stayed across town, he wouldn't get up until after nine, then he'd be behind and have very little time to work, shower, and get to the theater for rehearsal.

As the movie started up, Sawyer could picture Dad beside him, a bowl of popcorn and a package of Twizzlers between them. They'd watch the movie in silence, then later, they'd dissect every scene and talk about why it was so awesome. There at the end, when Dad had lost nearly all motor function, they couldn't even do that. It killed him seeing Dad like that, and to watch Mom take care of him while Sawyer felt the need to escape. So he'd left her to go it on her own way too many times.

"No wonder I avoided coming back as much as possible." Suddenly, Sawyer didn't feel like watching a movie. It was pathetic, but he wanted to have someone he could really talk to. Not Mom, because he didn't want to force her to relive it.

Sawyer glanced behind him, out the window for the second time that night. The lights in Brynn's place were out.

And it wasn't like she'd want to talk to him anyway.

Chapter Five

Brynn automatically looked up when the chime on the door rang out.

Mom walked in, pushing her sunglasses up on her head. "There's my girl. Have you and your brother forgotten where Dad and I live?"

Brynn walked around the counter and hugged her. "Sorry, Mom. It's been crazy busy this week." The coupon had worked almost too well. Traffic in the store was up, and she'd been late to rehearsal the past two days because she felt too guilty to leave Paul and Travis, the high school kid who worked a few nights a week, to help all the customers by themselves. Luckily, they'd finally hit the mid-morning lull.

Paul came from the back of the store where he'd been restocking fishing line. "Hey, Ma."

Mom put a hand on her hip. "I was just asking your sister why we never see you two anymore. Surely you can at least swing by for Sunday dinner."

Paul looked to Brynn—like she'd be able to get either of them out of it. Mom had come in to give them a guilt trip, and once you were on that trip, she didn't let up until you gave in. "Yeah, we'll be there," he said. "In fact…I might bring a date. If that's all right."

Mom's face lit up. "A date?" Her voice was in the dogs-only octave now. "Oh, Paul, that'd be wonderful. I can't wait to meet her."

"It's still early in the relationship, so keep it low-key, okay?"

The smile on Mom's face grew even bigger. Then she turned to Brynn. "What about you?" She brushed her fingers across the vintage floral comb Brynn had pulled her hair back with this morning. "One of the ladies in my knitting club has a son who just moved into town, and he sounds like a nice guy. I think he went out with Kayla Norman last weekend, but you're much cuter than she is."

"Competitive dating?" Brynn said. "No thanks, Mom."

Mom sighed. "Sometimes I worry I'll *never* have grandchildren. Guess that's what I get for taking so long to have you two."

Instead of engaging in that bomb of a statement, Brynn changed the subject. "Where's Dad?"

"Out fishing. Where else?" Mom frowned at the mounted TV. "Still playing the same boring shows, I see." She set her purse down on the counter and wandered farther into the store, probably to inspect everything, the way she did whenever she came in. It was like she didn't want to work here but didn't want to let go, either.

Brynn glanced at Paul. "You know she's going to make a huge deal about you bringing a date, right?"

He leaned against the counter. "I know."

"And who is this girl? Why haven't I met her?"

Before he could answer, Mom came back up front. "Think I'll stick around here for a bit. Could you use my help?"

"Actually, we could," Brynn said. "Especially around

closing. I can't be late to rehearsal again."

"Oh, by then I'll need to be home to cook dinner."

Great. So in other words, she was only going to be here when it was slow, which would give her time to interrogate Brynn about her lack of a dating life.

Mom scooted closer, and Brynn automatically braced herself. "I know you have some issue against being set up, hon, but there are lots of couples who never would've met if they hadn't gone on blind dates. It's how it's done now. And Judith's son sounds perfect for y—"

"There's a customer. I better go see if he needs help." Brynn had never been so happy to see a guy in a canvas fishing vest in her life. Except when she asked if he needed anything, he grunted a response about "just looking" and moved farther into the store.

"Well, if you have any questions…" Brynn decided to stay up front for a few minutes and restack the tackle boxes, even though they didn't need it. The last thing she wanted to do was deal with questions about her dating life right now. This week she'd been trying to avoid Sawyer while putting herself out there at the local spots in town, and all she'd learned was that she was excruciatingly bad at flirting and that the datable men were apparently not hanging out in the places she was.

"Brynn, hon?" Mom called from next to the register. "Did you mean to organize the lures like this? It seems like the chug bugs should be closer to the top."

Lord, give me strength. Brynn didn't know why Mom wouldn't go fishing with Dad. He asked every time—he always got this hopeful look in his eye, too—but she rarely went out with him anymore. Brynn certainly didn't love fishing like Paul and Dad did, but she liked to go now and then. And sure, sometimes when she'd been trapped on the boat for *hours*, she would look out at the lake and have this urge to make a swim for the shore, as if she were breaking out of prison. But she liked to think she'd sacrifice for the guy she loved. If she ever found him, that is.

Hopefully he'd be as understanding when it came to sitting through her plays or letting her go on and on about literature and how they just didn't make love stories like they used to.

"I'm going to go ahead and move them for you so people can actually find what they're looking for," Mom said.

I think I need to beg Dad to drag her onto the lake next time. Mom had always sighed a bit about the fishing, but she'd also gone out once in a while to be with Dad. Brynn couldn't remember the last time her dad's fishing adventure stories— signature fisherman exaggerations added in, of course—had included Mom. Come to think of it, Mom seemed to avoid any talk of fishing or Dad lately. In fact, whenever Brynn brought up either subject, Mom sidetracked the conversation. *What's up with that?*

"Brynn, honey?" Mom waved her closer. "Why don't you come over here so I can show you how to better organize these? That way I don't have to keep doing it for you." Brynn took a deep breath and let it out slowly. This was going to be a long day.

"Crapcrapcrap." Brynn took the corner way faster than she should've, causing the tires of her car to screech. She parked, shot out of the front seat, and headed to the back door. It was locked, of course. She knocked, waited a couple seconds, and then sprinted toward the front. While she hadn't spoken directly to Sawyer since the door incident, she'd heard the snide comment he made yesterday about her being late again.

She rushed into the auditorium and down the steps. By the time she got up front she was breathless. Everyone else was already onstage and Leo and Tony were running their scene as Algy and Jack.

"Nice of you to join us, *Cecily*," Sawyer said with a huff. "This is the third day in a row."

Brynn let out a breath. "I know. I'm sorry. I just—"

"Now that Cecily's here, we can pick up right before the engagement scene. Yesterday it was awful."

Damn, he was being so cold today. Calling her Cecily. And the way he was staring at her, eyes narrowed, the muscles in his jaw tight, made the spot between her ribs ache. She wanted to argue that there were plenty of scenes she—or Cecily—wasn't in, but she knew that didn't matter. She was in the proposal scene, and it did need the most help.

She hurried up the stairs and got into position in the middle of the stage. "Where are we starting from?" she whispered to Leo.

"So, my dear chap, where shall we start our journey from today?" Leo asked Sawyer, which was exactly what Brynn had been trying to avoid—the asking where to start, though she also liked to avoid Leo's *in character* questions as much as possible.

"How about when Cecily's telling him they're engaged? Actually, just after that, when she tells him about the broken engagement. That's where it went downhill yesterday. Yes, it's got to be funny, but you're actors. Act like you like each other."

"I do like Leo—er, Algernon," Brynn said before Leo could correct her. "I mean, not like that, but—"

"I know you can pull off pretending to like someone," Sawyer said. "But act like you *love* him. Make the audience feel it."

I know you can pull off pretending to like someone? What the hell? Was he taking about the scene? Was he implying that she'd only pretended to like him?

Determined to make everyone in the whole damn place feel it, she lifted her chin and stared into Leo's eyes. "Yes, you've wonderfully good taste, Earnest. It's the excuse I've always given for your leading such a bad life."

Judging from the transformation she'd seen of Sawyer's house this past week, he had wonderfully good taste, too. The porch had been transformed from old and broken to a white Victorian-style beauty, the kind she'd always loved. The scalloped edges at the top were perfection, and the new royal blue door with etched glass was lovely.

But she didn't think it was excuse enough to lead a bad life. Not that he was totally bad.

Brynn realized her attention had drifted to him and she quickly moved to her next line, lifting the box of letters to show Algernon. "And this is the box in which I keep all your dear letters."

"My letters!" Leo said, eyes going wide. "But, my own sweet Cecily, I have never written you any letters."

"You need hardly remind me of that, Earnest." Brynn gave a dramatic sigh. "I remember only too well that I was forced to write your letters for you..." She continued on, focusing on the words, her hand movements, all while trying to stare at Leo as if he hung the moon. They went through talking about their broken engagement, and then Leo was kneeling in front of her.

"What a perfect angel you are, Cecily."

"You dear romantic boy." She leaned down enough for Leo to kiss her, and she ran her fingers through his hair, like the stage directions said. She didn't even flinch at how much hair gel was in it, because that's how good of an actress she was right now. "I hope your hair curls naturally, does—"

"Cut, cut, cut!" Sawyer stood. "Was that supposed to be more passionate? Because it sucked."

Frustration ran through Brynn, making her grit her teeth.

Right now, she was sort of wishing Sawyer would go back to ignoring the play and typing away at his computer. Did he even know what the play was about? "This is supposed to be the 1800s. It can't be too passionate or it would seem inappropriate for the time."

The next instant Sawyer was charging up the steps to the stage. "I'm not saying it's got to be a kiss with tongue and groping—"

Brynn's face heated, and worse, she imagined kissing Leo with tongue and groping. Ew.

"—I'm saying you've got to look at each other like you're in love so the audience will want it to work out. Our *modern* audience." Sawyer shook his head. "You two don't have any chemistry. You've got to work on that. Now, take it again, from before the proposal."

It was impossible to concentrate with Sawyer standing right there, so close she could hear every shift of his body and feel his gaze on her like a weight. All her lines were swimming together. Finally, she cleared her throat and forced the words out. "It would hardly have been a really serious engagement if it hadn't been broken off at least once. But I forgave you before the week was out."

Leo knelt, told her she was an angel. She said her line, trying to peer into his soul like she wanted to be with him, and then Leo kissed her. And it was sloppier than usual. She did her best to not jerk back, though it was her first instinct.

"Okay, that was just…" Sawyer moved in front of her. He looked at the playbook, then lowered it by his side and stared into her eyes. The air thickened around them and she could feel every thump of her heart. "What a perfect angel you are, Cecily." He said it so tenderly, his smile close-lipped but full of joy.

"You dear romantic boy," she said, all out of instinct because thoughts were getting fuzzy.

He leaned in and kissed her, a soft kiss with his lips barely parted. Brynn's heart beat faster and her head swam. The pressure of his lips increased for a delicious moment, and then they were gone. A quick, simple kiss, but when his mouth left hers, she felt its absence so strongly that she couldn't think about anything else for a couple of seconds. Her breath was stuck somewhere in her lungs and her lips still tingled, living the sensation over and over again. Sawyer's eyes bored into her, and she swore there was desire playing in the green… Heat wound through her body, her hands itched to reach out and touch him. And then she remembered she was supposed to. She ran her fingers through his hair and felt the whisper of his breath on her wrist as he exhaled.

"Wow, that was good," Wendy said from the front, breaking Brynn from her trance.

Brynn stepped back and swallowed, but her throat wasn't working right. Sawyer's eyes never left hers, and one corner of his mouth curved up in a smug, self-satisfied way.

"It was all right, I suppose," Brynn said, working to keep her voice steady. She crossed her arms and shrugged. "For a first-timer, anyway."

That only made Sawyer's smile grow wider.

"But you didn't kneel," Leo said. "The stage directions clearly say kneel."

Sawyer turned to Leo, and he looked surprised to see him standing there. "I, uh, think you should stand to kiss her. It'll be less awkward and hopefully fix what's been missing. Let's at least try it."

Brynn couldn't help but watch Sawyer as he jumped off the stage, not bothering with the stairs. Funny how she'd dreamed of kissing him all the time in high school, but her fantasy wasn't even close to the real thing, and that was when the real thing was a quick fake kiss onstage. Her heart felt like it'd just been wrung out and shoved back in her chest.

Stupid emotions. Why were they doing this to her? Why did she want someone so badly whom she shouldn't want at all?

"Cecily?" Leo snapped his fingers in front of her face. "Don't you want to tell me about our broken engagement and how you forgave me?" Whenever they were onstage—or even off, actually—Leo insisted on calling her Cecily, just like he wanted to be called Algernon at all times. And that was fine. But for once, she didn't want to be a character who fell in love. She wanted to be Brynn, the girl who found the right guy and fell in love. But she pulled herself together and powered through.

And their scene *was* better. She was sure it had nothing to do with the fact that she closed her eyes and pretended it was Sawyer kissing her again.

Nope. Nothing at all.

• • •

Sawyer watched the scene play out, and while he kept telling himself Brynn and Leo were only actors, the muscles between his shoulder blades had gotten tighter with every take. He knew he could have no claim on Brynn, but he also knew he wanted one. While he'd been trying to prove a point with the scene, it'd taken all his control not to kiss her in a completely non-1800s-approved way.

And he sure as hell didn't want to watch Leo kiss her one more time. "Okay, let's move to the next scene."

They moved on to where Cecily and Gwendolyn met for the first time. The play was really starting to grow on him—the material, working on a scene and seeing it get better. Sawyer settled back in his seat, now used to the fact that there was hardly any padding in it.

As the director, he probably should be paying attention

to the entire scene, but he couldn't take his eyes off Brynn. Their eyes met and she quickly glanced away. Every time they were together, he thought things were going well. They'd talk, she'd smile—she had the perfect smile. Nice full lips that he now knew were as soft as they looked. He liked the sexy cat-eye thing she did with her makeup, too. Then there were her curves...

Sawyer's pulse cranked up and he took a drink from his water bottle in an attempt to cool down. Once he was in better control, he forced himself to watch the interchange between the Jack and Algernon characters.

He lasted a minute or two before he was staring at Brynn again. Looks aside, there was something about her. An infectious enthusiasm he wanted to catch. Even when she was mad at him, it was as if she wanted to be mean but simply didn't have it in her. Which was only more confusing—why was she working so hard to keep him away? He was trying to show her they could at least be friends, like with fixing her door all those nights ago.

I bet she had one of those disastrous relationships and now she's scared of getting close to anyone. He'd had a friend in college who was like that. The guy who liked her kept showing her she could trust him day after day, and now they'd been together for more than a year.

For a brief moment, he had the thought that he'd show Brynn she could trust him. But that was crazy, considering she was off limits and by the time she wasn't, he'd be headed back to New York anyway. He didn't want to make it worse for her when he left. Still, that kiss wouldn't leave his mind. There was a spark there, a desire he hadn't felt in a long time. He needed to at least talk to her, and this time, he wasn't going to take no for an answer.

When they got to the end of the second act, he stood. "I think that went pretty well. We'll start on the third act tomorrow."

Everyone started off the front of the stage, and Brynn headed in the other direction—trying to duck out the back again, no doubt. Sawyer charged up the stairs, against the flow of traffic, and slid behind the stage wagon with the garden scenery painted on it.

Good, from here, no one else should be able to see us, even if they haven't left the theater yet.

There she was, about to pass through the curtains.

"Brynn, wait! Come on, you can't avoid me forever."

She glanced over her shoulder at him, and her eyes widened. "I'm not. I've, uh, just gotta—"

He grabbed her hand to keep her from bolting, which was what it looked like she was about to do. "Tell me what's going on."

"I need to..." She gestured in the direction of the exit, but he could hear the breathlessness in her voice. His gaze lowered to her lips as she said, "Got somewhere...to be."

His brain told him to stop staring, to forget how nice it had been to kiss her. That this was a bad idea and he should turn right back around and go home before he made things worse. But she looked so tiny and vulnerable, and he wanted to feel that spark again.

He slid his arm around her waist and lowered his mouth to hers. Her hands came up between them on his chest, and he thought she was going to push him away. But then they slipped up around his neck as she parted her mouth under his.

Desire flared through him, and he couldn't suppress a moan at the way her body fit perfectly against his. He took his time exploring her lips, tasting her mouth, holding her tightly to him.

When she swirled her tongue around his, every thought he'd ever had disappeared.

Then she suddenly stepped back, the shock of going from a kiss like that to nothing a total jolt to his system.

"I can't do this. I need to go." She pulled at the curtain, but there was only more fabric. She ran her hand along it, obviously looking for where it split, which gave him just enough time to realize he needed to do something to stop her from leaving.

He put his hands on her waist and her posture stiffened. Not exactly what he'd been hoping for. "Hold up. I shouldn't have done that, I know. But I feel like I'm missing something every time I talk to you. Tell me what's going on."

"What's going on is that this was a mistake. Now please let me go."

He dropped his arms, trying not to let it show that he felt like he'd been punched in the gut.

She ran her hands over the velvet curtain again, still looking for the spilt. Managing to be adorable somehow, even as frustrated as he was with her. He was pretty sure that meant he'd already lost his mind over this girl.

She wasn't even close, so he reached over her and swept the fabric aside. She glanced back at him and his heart clenched.

Then she charged through the opening in the curtain and pushed out the back door, the noise clanging through the sudden quiet.

· · ·

"What the hell? I mean, seriously. What. The. Hell?" Brynn brought her shaky hand up to her still-burning lips. The romantic dreamer in her was having a hard time ignoring the fact that she'd *never* been kissed like that.

And she'd definitely never responded like that. All she'd been able to think in that moment was that she needed to be closer to Sawyer, even though every inch of her had already been pressed against him. Dani's words about how her heart told her she loved Wes before her brain did popped into Brynn's head, which so wasn't helpful right now. This wasn't her heart. Her heart said he'd hurt her before and she didn't want to risk it again.

But her lips, her body…they said they wanted more.

Bad idea was an extreme understatement. Especially since he'd asked her what was going on, his question making it clear he knew she wasn't being totally honest with him.

What am I going to do? How am I going to face him every day?

She rested her forehead on the steering wheel, the plastic hard against her skin. He was going to figure out she was the nerdy girl who'd asked him to prom, she just knew it. She shouldn't care—fine, let him know. She should shove that fact in his face so he could see what he missed out on all those years ago.

Only she didn't want him to know. She wanted him to wonder why she didn't like him, the same way she'd had to wonder about him back in high school. She wanted him to see what it was like to be rejected. Her chest burned, a toxic mix of resentment and hurt going through her. She pictured herself in the red, supposed-to-be-prom dress she'd made, the sleeves perfectly puffed to Regency-era perfection, the ruffled bodice with a satiny ribbon underneath. Spinning around her room as the skirt billowed around her, foolishly filled with hope.

She'd fantasized how the night would go—how people would gasp at the beauty of her dress like she did whenever she watched *Pride and Prejudice*, finally seeing her as a person they wanted to know. Especially since she'd be on Sawyer's arm.

Without a second thought, he'd ruined that possibility

and shattered her already fragile confidence.

He doesn't deserve to kiss me, and I'm never letting him do it again.

Brynn looked up in time to see Sawyer's familiar black car moving through the parking lot. She quickly fired up her engine and drove around the back of the theater, going the extra-long way to get to the road.

She wished that Sawyer had stayed in New York and away from her theater. Avoiding him wasn't working. She needed a replacement. One who was handsome and could kiss her hard enough to make her forget all about the guy who'd broken her heart when she was eighteen.

Chapter Six

Brynn had been psyching herself up for this conversation all morning, but it wasn't making it any easier to spit out the words. She'd almost started three times, but people had been coming into the shop and... Okay, she'd chickened out.

She finished replacing the receipt paper on the register and then turned to Paul. "I need dating advice. I know it's weird, and honestly, if I had anyone else to ask, I'd ask them. But I need help. For one, where do I even go to meet a guy? And then, how do I keep him?"

"Guys are like fish. You wave something shiny at them"—Paul waved one of the silver spinner lures—"and then once you get your hook in, you yank real hard and reel him in."

Brynn tilted her head and stared at him. "I'm serious."

"So am I. Here's the thing..." He looked at her and then shook his head. "Never mind."

"No, go ahead and say what you're going to say. I love putting on plays and it keeps me busy, but I wanna have someone to come home to someday." She swung her arms around. "I want to start living life."

Paul put his hands on her arms and slowly pushed them down. "You're just... You're like a hurricane. You come in talking a hundred miles an hour, swinging your arms around and saying things like 'living life.' You've gotta hold back when you first meet people. Ease them into the crazy."

Brynn's heart clinched. "Ouch."

"See, this is why I wasn't going to say anything."

She took a deep breath and pushed on. "No, I asked. But say I hold back the" —she swallowed past the ache in her throat—"crazy. There's still the problem of finding a guy. It's not like I'm going to meet anyone here. I'd never go for a fisherman, and obviously they don't like me anyway."

"Howard comes in all the time to see you," Paul said.

She scowled at her brother. "He's, like, seventy."

"More like sixty, and he's single." Paul waggled his eyebrows.

"Yay for me." She propped her elbow on the counter and dropped her chin into her hand.

Paul patted her shoulder and shot her a consoling smile. "You're a fun person, and you know I love you."

"But?"

"But sometimes when you start with the love stories, or you throw out a line from a play, no one knows what you're talking about. I've seen you totally crash and burn conversations with guys who were checking you out a few minutes before. And all that stuff's okay spread out over time. But you've got to leave a little mystery. Make them work to get to know you. And really, hold back on the play quotes as long as possible."

If the conversation continued on like this, she might have to mop her spirits off the floor. "So what am I supposed to talk about? Fishing? Then I'll be even weirder."

"Let him talk first. Act interested, but not too interested. Answer his questions with more than a yes or no, but keep it brief. And the less serious you seem about a relationship, the better. You hang out a couple times and make *him* think he wants to be in a relationship." Paul twisted the silver spinner so that it was hook-side up. "Then you've got him hooked and reeled in before he even realizes it."

"I suppose I bash him on the head to get him to stop flopping around and fighting it, too," Brynn said.

Paul laughed. "Probably wouldn't hurt. I think dragging him to your plays and quoting Shakespeare is about the same thing."

"You really do wonders for the self-esteem, you know that?" She'd expected him to tell her to find someone who understood her and liked the same things. Maybe get tips on where to find that guy. But she supposed this made sense, as much as she hated to admit it. She always said too much too fast. Except with Sawyer, and that was more because she'd tried to avoid talking to him as much as possible.

Oh my gosh, Paul's right. With Sawyer, I've held back, let him think I was some diva actress, pretended I don't care about him, and he's all about it. That's why he kissed me.

She straightened, resolve filling her. "I can do this. I can keep things light."

"It'd be better if you knew how to flirt. And before you ask, no, I can't teach you. You're my sister and it's weird. Maybe call Dani for that."

"I've seen you flirt, actually, and trust me, you're the last person I'd ask." She gave Paul's shoulder a playful shove.

He laughed, and she joined in. But then she caught movement by the front window, and she stared at the guy standing just outside, his hand on the door. It looked like... surely not. Fate wasn't that cruel, was it?

Apparently, it was, because Sawyer Raines was totally coming into the Bigfish Bait and Tackle. Brynn's pulse thundered through her ears. She couldn't face him. Not yet.

And not in here. "I have to go…get something!"

She tried to sneak out the back door, but she'd forgotten to unlock it this morning—which was a total fire hazard on top of being damned inconvenient. She didn't have the keys, either.

"What the hell are you doing?" she heard Paul say, but she ignored him, frantic for an escape. She glanced around and then ducked behind the shelf with the waders. Because if you were going to hide from someone, there was no better cover than rubber boots that go up to the armpit, right?

Man, up close, these things totally smell.

All her blood was rushing through her head as she heard Paul greet Sawyer and ask what he was looking for. *This is ridiculous. I should just stand up and tell him I work here.*

But then she'd have to talk to him, and she'd have to introduce Paul, and then all her lies—which were more like innocent miscommunications, really—would come undone. After all, Sawyer was the one who'd *assumed* she was from LA. She'd never said it.

Had she?

Crap, what if he recognizes Paul? He was a few years older than she was, so she doubted Sawyer would know him, and even if he did, he wouldn't realize he had a little sister in his class unless Paul brought it up, and why would he do that?

She leaned forward, even though her thighs were starting to burn, straining to hear what they were saying. "…thinking of doing some fishing from the shore," Sawyer said.

"Do you need a pole?" Paul asked.

Brynn glanced behind her at the poles and started praying he didn't. If he caught her back here, she'd just lie down and die. At least it would be a dramatic exit.

"No, I've got a good one."

I bet you do, she thought, her face heating even though she hadn't said it aloud. How mature was she? It was official.

She'd finally lost her mind, and it was all Sawyer's fault.

Her phone rang, and she swore as she scrambled to pull it out and shut it up. She hit answer and held her breath for a moment. When she was sure she was in the clear, she lifted the phone to her ear and whispered, "Hello?"

"Brynn? Why are you whispering?" It was Dani.

"Long story." Brynn cast another glance toward the register. She could make out Sawyer's feet and the low murmur of his and Paul's voices. Her brother glanced in her direction, forehead all scrunched up, and she shrank back farther. "What's up?"

"Turns out Wes does have a friend who's single. He's a cop, and he's helping Wes by going out and trying the adventure tours with him, making sure they're in the clear, legal-wise and such. He's super hot, too. I was thinking it'd be fun to all get together so you could meet."

A sliver of hope shone through. Cop. Hot. What more could she ask for? "Yeah. Sounds good."

"Cool. I wanted to check with you before setting it up. I'll see when he's free and call you once I have the details."

Brynn disconnected the call and slid the phone back into her pocket. Suddenly everything Paul said hit her, and her stomach rolled over. She'd probably ruin her chances with the prospective guy within a few minutes of their date—she'd never been good under pressure, and she was even worse if there was a cute guy involved. *I might as well call off the date now. Save myself another hit to my dissipating ego.*

She heard the ding of the register opening, and then, a moment later, the chime over the door. Footsteps approached and then Paul was staring down at her, arms crossed. "Didn't we just have a talk about not acting crazy? That's the first guy not in the senior-citizen-discount age to come by in a while, and you're back here hiding."

"That was the director of my play."

Paul glanced over his shoulder.

She inched closer to the boots. "He's not still here, is he?"

"No, but he seemed like a nice enough guy. I don't get why you'd hide from him."

Well, he kissed me yesterday, and I liked it. That sounded straitjacket insane, so she shrugged. "He sorta thinks I'm from LA."

Paul raised an eyebrow. "You told him that?"

"Not exactly. He assumed and I just...let him. A few minutes ago, you told me I needed to not be myself."

"I said hold back. I'm not even sure *what* you're doing."

Brynn used the shelves to pull herself up. "I'm surviving." She thought about telling Paul the truth. He'd never understood how hard high school had been for her, but when she'd told him the occasional story here and there, he'd actually gotten pissed that people had treated her the way they did. So she didn't want to get into that, and she didn't want to explain, and she wasn't sure how her life had ended up in this weird place.

"If it's that bad, maybe you should quit the play," Paul said.

"No, I'm fine, really." What she needed was for the cop guy to be as interested in her as Sawyer seemed to be right now.

So how do I pull that off, with me being me?

A crazy idea started to form. Apparently acting like someone else was working with Sawyer, and according to her brother—and her dismal lack of a dating life—she needed to learn how to flirt. This could be the perfect opportunity. When Sawyer acted interested, she could see what worked and what didn't. If he stopped talking to her, then fine, it'd make rehearsals easier. But if it worked, she'd know what to do when she met the right guy. It'd be like the ultimate dress rehearsal. "Actually, I've got everything under control."

• • •

This was out of control. Sawyer was watching out his window for Brynn to come home, because apparently he was a masochist who enjoyed being dissed by the same girl over and over again. He couldn't help himself, though. Kissing her had awakened a part of him he'd forgotten existed, and he wanted to see where it went, even if common sense told him to let it go.

Besides, his arms ached from all the work he'd been doing on the house, and he needed a break. So he'd pulled his old fishing pole out of Mom's garage and bought bait. At first he was going to go out alone—he probably should—but then he got this idea that he'd show Brynn they could hang out as friends, and then she'd see how much fun he could be. And then eventually, he could kiss her again.

Damn, he wanted to kiss her again.

Just when he was about to give up, her blue Camry pulled up. He grabbed the trash bag for an excuse to be outside and headed out the back door.

"Hey." He could actually feel his pulse pounding in his neck. He couldn't remember the last time he'd been this nervous. Or the last time he'd just jumped in without fully thinking things through. He forced his limbs to move forward and toss the bag of trash in the Dumpster. "About yesterday…" He considered saying he was sorry, but he wasn't, and he didn't want her to take it as an insult. Shit, he should've planned this out better.

She kicked the grass with the toe of her shoe. "Let's not talk about yesterday."

Fine by him. "So, I was about to head down to the lake for some fishing, and I think you should come with me."

She glanced at her house, and he sensed he was losing her.

"Just two friends hanging out," he said. She slowly turned back to him, and his gaze drifted toward her lips. He was going to have to avoid looking at them if he was going to get through this act-like-friends thing. "I've got a spare pole and everything we'll need…"

The breeze stirred her hair, sending strands of it into her face. She swept it back and tucked it behind her ear. "Okay. Let me change clothes and feed my birds first."

"Birds?"

"You know, little feathered creatures with beaks and wings?"

He smiled. He shouldn't like that she was mocking him, but it sent warmth through his chest—yep, total masochist, because he wanted more. "Need any help?"

"No thanks. I'll only be a minute." She disappeared into her house, and he went to grab the equipment. So, friends… He could ask her about LA. Where she went to school, things like that. Oh, and he could show her how to fish. Friends put their arms around each other when they showed them things, right?

Well, this friend was going to, anyway.

• • •

"What do you think, guys?" Brynn asked her parakeets, spinning for them to show off the pink and white sundress she'd thrown on. "Does this say I'm a city girl who is only moderately interested in what you do or say?"

Lancelot ignored her, but Guinevere chirped.

"Good enough for me." She definitely wouldn't mention the fact that she talked to her birds—she knew that much even without Paul's help. But she kept what her brother had said in mind. Stick with light topics and conversation. No quotes from plays or books or movies. Interested, but not too interested.

Maybe I'll try a flirty smile. She backed up so she could see into her mirror and attempted a couple, then decided she should keep her lips pressed together. Smiling made her cheeks stand out and gave her a total chipmunk look. No wonder that'd never worked before.

And now I'm psyching myself out. She slid on her sunglasses. That was better. She put her hand on the doorknob and told herself this was like any other dress rehearsal. You saw what worked, what didn't, then you made notes and tried it again. It was okay if she bombed it.

Only then she opened the door and Sawyer was standing there holding fishing gear. She desperately wanted to prove she could play it cool with a guy like him. Never mind the fact that his grin sent her stomach up near her throat.

"Ready?" he asked.

Probably not. But here goes nothing, anyway. "Lead the way."

They walked the short distance to the shore together, and while Brynn's first instinct was to fill the silence, she kept her mouth closed. Instead she focused on the light breeze cooling off the heat of the day and stirring up the scent of clover and the mossy smell from the lake. Most importantly, she was waiting for Sawyer to take the lead in the conversation and see if this way of doing things actually worked.

Sawyer set his fishing gear in the grass. He didn't say a word as he got the pole ready, giving her time to study his profile and the way the muscles on his forearms stood out as he put the Scum Frog on the end of the line.

Not like that kind of thing impressed her. Much.

"This one's for you." He extended the fishing pole to her. She took it, but instead of moving away as she'd expected, he stayed right next to her. "Summer's a good time for top-water baits." He lifted the hook with the little frog-looking lure on top. "These are called Scum Frogs. They're good for fishing in places other lures can't go without snagging on moss, around the weeds and lily pads, for example."

Brynn smiled. "Ooh. Nice name."

"Most lures have goofy names."

You're telling me. She wrinkled her forehead, like this was all news to her. "But fish would actually eat a frog?"

"The big fish do, and that's what we're trying to catch."

She grinned at him. "The big fish. Of course."

The ditzy act was actually working. He was so proud to explain to her something that she'd learned when most girls were playing dress-up princesses.

"Okay, so casting is a bit tricky."

There was acting, and then there was straight-up lying. Brynn figured this landed in column B. "Actually, I do know how—"

He put his arms around her, one hand on her hip and the other moving down her arm to the hand holding the fishing pole. "What was that?" he asked, his breath against her temple. She could feel the heat coming from him, not to mention the hard muscles underneath his clothes, and suddenly, she *didn't* remember how to cast.

"Where do I put my hand again?" Okay, any minute he was going to call her out.

"Hold this button down with your thumb. We're going to swing it back…" He guided her arm and his fingers gripped her waist tighter. Heat was spreading from his touch, winding its way through her body. "Then we'll swing it forward and let go of the button. Ready?"

She nodded. He started to move her hand forward and she hit the release button way too early. Hey, if she was going to act, she might as well go all out.

She faked a pout. "Guess I'll be catching all the fish that swim in the grass." She looked over her shoulder at him, and he was so close she could see the stubble along his jaw and his pulse beating at the base of his neck. She licked her lips. "I think you're going to have to show me again."

Keeping his arms around her, he reeled in the line. "Don't worry, it sometimes takes a couple of tries, even for people who've been doing it for a while."

Brynn bit back a smile. All this time, she'd been wracking her brain, trying to figure out how to get a guy, but ruining it by talking about things like acting. Who knew that all she needed to do was to use her performance skills *on* them?

On the second cast, she let go at the right time.

Sawyer squeezed her shoulder. "A little early, but that's okay. It's hard to cast that far at first."

Early, my ass. That's where I want it, right in the lily pads. But she didn't say that. She held back, just like Paul told her to, sticking to smiling and blinking.

"Now slowly reel it in, so it looks like a frog moving over the water, and hope a big bass comes to take a bite." Sawyer picked up his fishing pole and cast his own line—too far, because he was obviously trying to show off. When he moved closer to her, she didn't move away, even though their lines were probably going to get tangled.

He grinned and nudged her with his elbow. "Fun, huh?"

It was impossible not to return his smile. "Totally." Oh yeah, she was *totally* rocking the LA girl persona now.

"So, tell me about living in Los Angeles."

"I…really can't describe it." *Literally.* Well, she supposed she could go with the generic things she got from watching movies and television. "It's…sunny. There's the beach. Palm trees. The Hollywood sign. Rodeo Drive. Movie stars. Smog and traffic. Yep, good ol' LA."

He stopped reeling in his line and studied her, so intently she was glad for the sunglasses, because it seemed like he'd see into her soul otherwise, and it'd definitely tell him she was a big fat liar. "And if I said I was thinking about moving there, what would you say?"

She focused on the familiar feel of the weight of her line, how it skipped and bumped through the weeds but didn't tug enough for it to be a bite from a fish. "I guess that depends on why you want to go there."

He looked out at the water for a moment, the setting sun giving his profile a golden glow. "One of my screenplays got made into a movie—and it was amazing seeing my story on the big screen, something I've dreamed about for years. Even though it's done well and there's interest in the one I'm writing now, it's still a very competitive career, and according to my agent it'd be good for me to move to LA and"—he made air quotes—"'immerse myself.'"

"Immerse yourself. That sounds…" She stopped before she said, *Sounds like a life I'd hate but good luck with that.* Because it wasn't about her, and she wasn't supposed to be overly opinionated, but should be turning it back on him. "Is that what you want? To be one of those LA guys who talk movie biz? Name drops and drives a Porsche and that kind of thing?"

"I wouldn't say no to a Porsche."

Brynn laughed. "Well, you'd definitely fit in with all the pretty people."

Sawyer raised an eyebrow, and a smug smile curved his lips. Oops. That slipped through the filter. This was supposed to be the wave-the-sparkly-lure-at-him time, not… Okay, she so wasn't going into that analogy right now. But she was fairly sure he was still interested.

Her hook came up, and she cast it again, sloppier than she usually did—sloppy enough her dad would've had a stroke over how he'd failed as a teacher—and started the process of reeling it in. "So you didn't answer the question. Is moving to California what you want?"

Sawyer recast his line—in the same too-far spot. "What I want is to write movies that make people laugh, cry, grip the edge of their seat. Whatever reaction, I want it to be big. To make an impact." He ran his thumb over the handle of the fishing pole. "Cheesy, right?"

She couldn't keep from reaching out and giving his wrist a quick squeeze. "Not at all."

It was a good thing he was just her practice boyfriend and she was lowering her expectations, because otherwise she'd think this was one of those moments where they had a deep connection and everything would be forever changed between them.

"So, why'd you— I think I got something." He jerked up the pole and sure enough, the end was bent and the line tight. Her line was still slack, blowing in the breeze, so she was extra glad she hadn't said anything about him casting too far out. She scooted away from him so their lines wouldn't tangle.

"You wanna reel it in?" he asked.

"You go ahead. You caught it."

"No, seriously, drop your pole and get over here. I'll help you."

Well, if he was going to help her… She set down her pole and moved toward him. He put both arms around her and let her take over reeling it in. "Spin it as fast as you can. He's hooked good, so don't give him any slack."

The fish was fighting hard, and it was obviously a big one. Her arms started burning from the exertion.

"You got it," he said, his lips right by her ear. When the large bass finally came out of the water, she couldn't help but squeal like it was actually her first time catching a fish. She glanced over her shoulder to find him grinning back at her.

And it took everything in her to keep from dropping the pole and kissing him again.

"So how'd you like your first time fishing?" Sawyer asked after walking her to her front door.

It was way too late to clarify that she'd been fishing multiple times and knew enough about bait and lures to star on her own fishing show.

Sawyer's eyebrows rose, and she realized she still needed to answer. Since she was trying not to be a complete liar, she went with, "I had a nice time fishing with you."

Usually this would be the part where she waxed poetic about the breeze carrying the scent of flowers and the glittering lake, and how she didn't want it to end. But she stopped herself. She needed to maintain an air of mystery. This method was taking some getting used to, but it was actually working. Sawyer was leaning in, his hand gripping the doorframe, his gaze fixed on her lips.

"Well, I'll see you later," she said, pulling away. Hopefully leaving him wanting more.

"Maybe next time we can rent a boat and take it out on the lake. Or if you're done with fishing, we could do something else…" He shot her a smile that made the rest of the world fade to gray.

Danger. This was the point where she could turn back into her usual babbling self if she wasn't careful. *Focus, Brynn, focus. Cool. Indifferent.* "Maybe."

She closed her door, waited five whole seconds, and then did a celebratory dance. She did it! She'd actually pulled it off.

Chapter Seven

Drawn by the scent of brewing coffee, Sawyer padded into the kitchen, squinting against the light.

"I'm about to make some eggs," Mom said, pulling a carton out of the fridge. "You want bacon, too?"

"Do you even have to ask?" He got out a mug and filled it with coffee. After a couple of nights sleeping at the house, he'd decided he needed a solid eight hours on a comfy mattress, so he'd come back to Mom's. It'd taken him forever to fall asleep, though, because he kept picturing Brynn out by the lake, her thin cotton dress blowing in the breeze. He replayed having his arms around her, and then he was coming up with ideas to get her to go out with him again. He'd never be able to keep from kissing her next time, especially if she was going to smile at him the way she had yesterday.

"You look happy this morning." Mom put several strips of bacon into the skillet.

"It's a good morning." He'd forgotten what it was like to wake up looking forward to the day instead of planning ways to get through it. How addictive it was, that desire to see another person, before it got messed up and overly complicated. Even though he knew it couldn't last forever, he was going to let himself enjoy it for a few hours before he screwed it up with thinking. "By the way, there's a bass in the fridge. I caught it yesterday and thought maybe we'd have it for dinner tonight or tomorrow."

What was really crazy was he wanted to ask Brynn to come over. He could say that she needed to taste the fish she caught. But that was a bad idea. Mom would start expecting him to stay, and he had no doubt she'd instantly get attached to Brynn. Not to mention it would probably scare Brynn away.

But maybe he could swing by her place later. Or maybe he should play it cool and wait to talk to her tomorrow at rehearsal. Tomorrow night suddenly seemed so far away, though.

"How's the house coming?" Mom asked. "Are you sure we don't need to hire someone to help you?"

"I'm sure. I'm enjoying doing it, actually." He took a sip of coffee. "Everything's in the transitioning stage, but I'll start on new flooring next week. I was hoping you'd go with me to help pick it out. Make sure it's something you like."

Mom waved a hand through the air. "It doesn't matter what I like."

"Still. I could use your help." Sawyer took in the faded wallpaper and the linoleum from the eighties. "I could help you fix up this place, too, if you wanted."

"Oh, I don't need anything fancy."

Once again, Mom was putting everything she wanted last. It was why the lake house never got renovated until now, for someone else, instead of years ago, for her. "I'm not saying fancy, but just a little update. Whatever you want."

"Why don't you look for a place that you'd like instead? There are some nice homes that recently went up for sale a few streets over. Or if that's too close to me, then the east side is nice. And when you think about it, it's kind of silly to put so much work into the lake house only to turn around and sell it when you could—"

"Mom…you know I'm not staying. This isn't my home anymore. New York is." He'd said it without thinking, because that was how he felt. But since he was trying to sell the California idea—to her and to himself—he added, "Or possibly Los Angeles, if that's where I need to go for my career."

Mom didn't say anything, but her shoulders tensed. She cracked the eggs so hard he was pretty sure there'd be shells in the pan. "I thought you could write from anywhere."

"Me, too, but if there's more opportunity…" He didn't want to say much else because he knew they'd simply talk in circles, the way they seemed to whenever this subject came up.

"Is it so bad that I want you to settle down? Start a family?"

Was it so bad that he didn't want those things? She'd definitely say yes.

Mom clung to family life, to being here, like she needed and cherished the memories. When Sawyer looked around, though, he only remembered the bad. That last part of his senior year, when it was clear Dad wasn't going to hold on much longer and Mom had to do everything for him, from feeding him to taking him to the bathroom. Earlier that year Sawyer had football to distract him, but right before graduation, he stopped going to class, and when he actually went, he was outlining in his notebook. That was when he'd written his first screenplay. It was full of awful lines and had no plot, but it'd been the perfect escape. So when Dad died a few months later, Sawyer jumped at the chance to get away from this place. He'd moved to New York and worked at odd jobs until he finally got accepted to the New York Film Academy. And he'd never looked back.

He didn't have the desire to get married and have kids, and he wanted it even less after his last relationship.

But none of that would make Mom feel better—in fact, it'd crush her. So he set down his mug and tried to sound as though having a family might be in his future someday. "I'm only twenty-five, Mom. Don't worry; I've got time for all that other stuff later."

"You never know how much time you have," she said.

There was nothing he could really say to that. But it did make him realize Mom was right about limited time. So screw playing it cool. Sawyer wanted to spend every second he could with the girl who'd made him fall asleep with a smile on his face.

• • •

On Sundays, the bait and tackle shop opened an hour early— at seven instead of eight—and closed at four instead of six. Since her family's only religion was fishing, Brynn used to think that was why. But now she suspected Mom was just that serious about everyone sitting down for Sunday dinner. In the past hour alone, she had sent no less than ten texts, everything from asking about wine choices, to salad dressings, to what exact time Brynn was getting there, and did Paul know that dinner was starting at five sharp?

"I'm sure you've texted him a hundred times to remind him," Brynn muttered. She wasn't sure what was going on with Mom, but she was taking stressing over dinner to a whole new level. Apparently she wanted to make a *really* good impression on Paul's new girlfriend.

I still can't believe I haven't gotten any of the info on this girl. She would've bugged Paul about her this morning, but he'd called in, asking if she and Travis could handle the store without him today.

He hadn't taken a day off in weeks, so of course she'd told him it was no problem. And it wasn't. It'd been slow, and they'd done most of the closing jobs already.

"Should I flip the sign to closed?" Travis asked.

Brynn glanced at the clock. Four on the dot. "Yeah, and the place is clean already, so you can go ahead and leave. I'll take care of everything else."

Travis grabbed the bag of lures he'd bought at a deep discount and his fishing pole from the back and headed out the back door, on his way to the lake, no doubt. Brynn changed the channel on the TV to a music station, ejected the cash register drawer, and got to work closing out for the day.

Like the theater, the empty fishing store held a hint of magic. But instead of stories to be told about love and tragedy, there were possibilities of record-breaking fish and tales of the one that got away.

A package with a Scum Frog popper caught her eye, and Brynn picked it up and smiled. Maybe there *were* possibilities of love stories behind some of the lures here.

Only I'm just supposed to be practicing how to fall in love. A knot formed in her gut. She tossed the lure aside and tried to focus on numbers, but she ended up having to recount the credit card receipts twice.

Finally, she got everything closed down and then headed to her car, thinking she'd get to Mom and Dad's with five minutes to spare.

Her phone chirped and she groaned. When she read the message, though, her stomach sank.

You did get the dessert, right?

She'd meant to pick up the cake from the bakery first thing that morning, but she'd gotten distracted thinking about the cute guy she went fishing with yesterday and automatically drove to the store.

Mom's going to kill me. Brynn glanced at her car and then down the street, where the bakery sat. It was at that three-block-away mark where it was almost silly to drive and almost silly not to. The street looked pretty crowded, though—apparently there were lots of people out and about this Sunday evening. Not wanting to waste even more time looking for parking, she hurried down the sidewalk. She made it two blocks, then had to stop for the red light.

She heard a tapping noise. Then it got louder. She glanced around, trying to find the origin. Then she spotted Sawyer sitting in the corner of the Daily Grind Coffee Shop, knocking on the window.

The pedestrian crosswalk sign flashed from red to white, but walking away from Sawyer felt rude—regardless of the fact that he'd done it to her before.

If she blew him off now, though, she might not get another chance to practice her flirting on him. It had worked like a charm yesterday, giving her a much-needed ego boost, and she was curious if she could keep it up. Practice makes perfect, and there was a date with a hot cop on the line, after all.

Brynn moved closer to the window and waved, flashing him what she hoped was an alluring grin. Sawyer held up a finger in the universal sign for hold on. He twisted back to his table, where she saw he had a laptop, notebook, and large coffee cup. He scribbled something on his notebook, ripped out the sheet of paper, and then held it against the window. In big block print it said CALL ME and then had his number underneath.

She dialed it, feeling silly standing outside the window calling him while he was right there, only a thick pane of glass away. "Call you now?" she asked when he answered.

"No, call me later. Get in here now."

"I can't. I'm late for…" Crap. If she told him she was late

for family dinner, then that would undo all of her—she still didn't want to call them lies. More like her carefully crafted character. Yeah, that sounded better.

"Stop trying to think of an excuse," Sawyer said, his deep voice soothing and undoing her at the same time. "You already took too long for me to believe any lame excuse you'd come up with now. It's starting to give me a complex, actually, and I can't write when I feel like that. Since you're the cause, you need to get in here and fix it."

"But I—"

He hung up the phone, crossed his arms, and stared at her. She so didn't have time for this, but she couldn't exactly walk away. Her phone chimed with another text from Mom.

Brynn glanced toward the bakery and then back at Sawyer. He frowned, a dramatic, made-for-the-stage kind of frown. And here she'd thought he was a serious guy. With a sigh, she backtracked to the coffee shop door, took a moment to inhale the delicious rich scent inside, and moved to where Sawyer was seated. The chair across from him scooted out— he'd obviously pushed it with his foot—and he gestured for her to sit down.

Brynn twisted the bauble ring on her finger. "I really do have somewhere I need to be. In fact, I'm super late, and I shouldn't have even come in here in the first place."

"What do you want? I'm on my third cup of coffee, so I'm thinking it might be time to switch to something else." He stood, so close their bodies were all but touching, and she wondered just how angry her mom would be if she skipped tonight's dinner.

Probably somewhere between nuclear and apocalyptic fall-out.

Her phone dinged. "One second." Mom. Of course. At times like these, she wished she hadn't insisted her mom learn to text. Then again, she'd be calling otherwise.

Brynn sent a quick text back telling Mom that she was running a little late but would be there ASAP. Mom's reply asked where Paul was and why he wasn't there yet, so she sent another text explaining she didn't know, but she knew he was coming.

When she glanced up from her phone, she noticed something in Sawyer's eyes—she swore he was looking at her like she was...pretty. Her heart swelled and she got that fresh-off-a-roller-coaster feeling. Everyone else—every*thing* else—disappeared.

Her hand moved to his face like it had a mind of its own. She ran her palm down his stubbled cheek. "You look nice. Very writerly."

He grinned. "You look nice, too. Very..." His eyes ran down her, burning every spot they touched. "I don't even know the right word. And I use words all day."

She laughed. "Whereas the rest of us don't?"

He slipped his hands behind her waist, pulling her to him. She could feel the heat coming off him, and it was distracting to say the least. "Ah, back to mocking me again. You think I'm just going to let you get away with that?"

Her heart pounded against her rib cage, and being this close was making her lightheaded in a way that made clarity seem overrated. "You walked right into it. Really, you only have yourself to blame."

Her phone dinged again, vibrating in her pocket. "I'm sorry, but I've gotta go." She reluctantly pulled away, hating how cold she suddenly felt without her body pressed against his. And for a crazy moment, she considered asking him to come to dinner. Confessing everything and turning whatever this was between them into a real possibility.

But then she remembered the only reason he was this interested was because she'd been pretending to be someone else whenever she was around him. And according to what he said yesterday, he wasn't even sure he was staying here permanently. In a way, that might be good. If she crashed and burned during this dating test-run—which, let's face it, wouldn't be all that surprising—he'd leave again, taking her humiliation with him.

Still, she couldn't get over the way he was smiling at her, genuine happiness swimming in his green eyes. How his hand drifted back to her waist, as though he couldn't help himself.

He seems…like he might seriously be interested. In me.

Now she was imagining things. Dreaming them up like she always did, making every gesture mean more than it did. He didn't care about her. She was a mystery, like Paul told her to be. It was possible he was only looking for a temporary girl while he was here, and she happened to be the closest.

"I'll catch you later," she said as though she didn't care either way.

"You have my number," he said as she retreated. When she glanced back, he was still watching her like there wasn't anyone else in the room.

Mom swung open the door and threw her arms around Brynn, nearly crushing the Double Chocolate Dream Cake between them. "Goodness gracious, I thought you must've gotten into an accident on your way here, you took so long."

Ah, hugs and a guilt trip, all at the same time. That's motherly love for you.

Brynn patted Mom's back. "I'm fine. And I'm sorry I'm late. Is Paul here yet?" This was a win-win question because if he was, Mom would stop focusing on how Brynn was late, and if he wasn't, Mom would focus on how *he* was late.

"Yes, he and Carly got here a couple minutes ago. Didn't you get my text?"

You texted me? she wanted to say with a good dose of sarcasm, but instead said, "I don't text and drive— Wait. Who did you say Paul was with?"

"Brynn. Hey." Paul came into the room hand in hand with a girl. Not just any girl. The name had instinctually triggered warning bells, but seeing her in the flesh was worse. Carly Johnson had been Sawyer's girlfriend most of senior year until she dumped him in front of everyone in one of those dramatic cafeteria room displays. Brynn remembered that moment, feeling sorry for Sawyer, but also inwardly celebrating her chance to finally lay it all on the line and ask him out.

Carly tilted her head, two tiny creases forming between her eyebrows. "Have we met before? You look kind of familiar." She was still beautiful, flawless tan skin, platinum blond hair, and the perfect big-boobs-to-small-waist combo. Like a Barbie on crack. It was so unfair. Couldn't the universe restore some balance? Give her a fat ass or something? "You went to Hough High, right?"

Yeah, get there faster. We both went there. You lived the dream version of high school, while I got to live the horror one. It was one thing for her to have been with Sawyer, but there was no way Brynn was going to let Carly have her brother.

"You used to have, like, light brown hair, though," Carly said. "And you always wore those cool, funky clothes."

Was she being passive aggressive? Was *cool, funky clothes* code for weird?

"Apparently, she's forgotten how to speak." Paul snapped his fingers in front of Brynn's face.

Brynn slapped them away. "Yep, that was me. And you were on the cheerleading team." She wished she'd stayed for that cup of coffee with Sawyer. Only now she was looking at Carly and thinking she couldn't compete with that, and there was no way he'd ever settle for a girl like her.

All the self-esteem her brief encounter with Sawyer had built deflated, leaving a too-thick feeling in her gut.

"You never told me you were a cheerleader," Paul said, kissing Carly's cheek. And she giggled. Actually *giggled*.

Mom beamed, unborn grandchildren dancing in her eyes. "Aren't they cute?"

Brynn forced her lips into a smile. "Super cute."

During dinner, she had to endure more of the *cuteness*. Paul and Carly, smiling and kissing and complimenting each other every second. For once, it wasn't giving Brynn a contact love-high.

Apparently, Carly had gone to cosmetology school and now worked at a salon. "Love that color and cut, by the way," she said, pointing at Brynn.

It would be easier to keep hating her if she stopped being nice. Or was she just *acting* nice? Either way, Carly was sure charming her parents and brother. The only consolation was that Brynn hadn't lost her mind and invited Sawyer—that would've been a whole new level of awkward. Or maybe they'd rekindle in front of everyone, and the day could finish going straight to hell.

After dinner, when Brynn found herself alone in a room with Carly, the girl turned to her and smiled. "I'm so glad I ran into you again."

Ran into… Bombarded my family. Same difference.

Carly's pouty lips stuck out farther. "I always felt so bad for you."

Pity. Yeah, that's super for my already dying self-esteem, so thanks for that.

Carly twisted the ends of her hair around her finger. "Getting de-pantsed in front of the whole school like that probably felt like the end of the world, but I'm sure no one really remembers it."

Right. That's why you're talking about it this very second.

And it wasn't de-pantsed. It was de-skirted. Just like that, there was the incident Brynn tried to avoid thinking about, flashing through her mind as if it were yesterday.

The school had called the dress rehearsal an assembly and required all students to go, so that the drama club would have an audience to practice on. Brynn was making her acting debut, a tiny part in a short scene. Mid-scene, a guy named Mark had stepped on her skirt. Only Brynn didn't know it, so she stepped forward like the stage directions told her to, and down came her skirt. First she had to worry about not tripping, what with the fact her ankles were bound. Once she got her balance, she had to shove a stunned-looking Mark *off* her skirt before she could pull it up. The audience had erupted in laughter, and she'd run off the stage, embarrassment burning every inch of her body.

Thinking of it again sent a wave of nausea rolling through her stomach.

But it didn't end there. No. The next day all anyone called her was McFlasher. People finally knew her name—enough to turn McAdams into McFlasher. What an honor.

"Really, I always thought it was cool you had your own thing going," Carly continued, as though she hadn't just brought up the worst moment of Brynn's life. There was still a part of her that relived it every time she went onstage, but she'd told herself she was strong enough to get over it. Five minutes ago, she would've said she was doing a hell of a job.

Carly sighed and put her hand on Brynn's knee. "I had way too many supposed friends who weren't true friends. I wish I'd hung out with more people like you."

Did she actually just say "people like you"?

"Excuse me. I've gotta go see if my mom needs help." Brynn ran into Paul on the way to the kitchen.

"So, Carly's great, huh?" he asked, Cheshire cat grin on his face.

"I knew her in high school."

"So?"

"So, that says it all."

Of course he didn't get it. Paul had been popular in high school. He was coordinated and confident and all the things that Brynn wasn't back then. She was about to launch into her monologue on why high school sucked—she had one all ready to go, too—but then Paul said, "Was she one of the people who was mean to you?" Disappointment was thick in his voice, and she could see it on his face as well.

"Not exactly. She was just..." *Dating my boyfriend. My pretend boyfriend.* Jealousy burned through Brynn's gut, even stronger than it used to when she saw Carly and Sawyer together in high school. Paul was staring at her, obviously waiting for more. "We hung in different circles, that's all."

Relief washed over his features. He really liked her, and he hadn't been interested in anyone since Skanky McSkankerson cheated on him and broke his heart.

Brynn pushed back the past that seemed determined to haunt her lately. "She's very pretty. Plus she's obviously crazy about you." And as much as she wished it were anyone but Carly Johnson, it was nice to see Paul happy. So Brynn put on another act and smiled so hard her cheeks hurt.

All the world's a stage, and all the men and women merely players...

Chapter Eight

As soon as Sawyer saw Brynn on the other side of the door, he was glad he'd decided to come back to the lake house. He'd told Mom he needed to get an early start in the morning, which was partially true, but he'd been hoping to see Brynn. He just thought he'd have to wait until tomorrow.

She looked different than she had earlier that day, but he couldn't pinpoint how. She seemed…deflated, almost. She twirled a piece of hair around her finger, her eyes not meeting his. "So…I felt bad about running out on you earlier today—"

"As you should." Sawyer reached out and squeezed her hand so she'd know he was kidding.

Her fingers slowly curled around his and his heart rate kicked up a couple notches. She wasn't pulling away. She was standing on his porch, the light from inside the house illuminating her features. She had a unique brand of pretty that was all her own, and he felt a little intoxicated as he took her in. Big eyes, perfect lips…

He swallowed. "You wanna come in for a bit?"

She glanced toward her house, and he worried she'd say

no. But then she nodded and stepped inside, pausing long enough for him to get a whiff of her floral scent. Her hand was still in his, too, and he was in no hurry to let it go.

Okay, Raines, just play it cool. Don't scare her off now that you've got her here. He shook his head. That made him sound like a serial killer. *I should use something like that in my screenplay, though. The bad guy's been such a hard character to nail down.*

She smiled at him and all work thoughts left his head. He scrambled to think of an excuse to keep her there for a while. "How about a movie? It's the greatest movie of all time, and also the only one I've got."

Her smile widened, showing off her cute cheeks. "Sounds like a win all around."

"Wait here. I'll get something for us to sit on."

Sawyer grabbed the sleeping bag and the spare blanket he'd been using and brought them out to the living room. He placed them down in front of the TV. "Sorry. Since I'm in the middle of remodeling the place, I don't have much furniture."

"No big deal. I like picnic movie time. Only I guess it'd need to have food to be a picnic. Not that I'm asking for food...I'm full, actually." She shook her head and then flopped down on the blanket. "Yeah, this is good."

No, it wasn't good. It was going to be uncomfortable if they didn't have something to rest against. He thought maybe he should suggest her place, but that might seem pushy or suggestive, and he didn't want to screw it up now that she was here. He spotted the box with the new cabinets inside and scooted it over to where he'd set up the blankets. "We'll use this for a backrest."

She leaned against it, and from this viewpoint, he had a good shot of her cleavage. Then he was thinking of that day she'd been changing in the car and her pink bra—

"Sawyer?"

He straightened, guilt flushing his skin. "Want a drink? I have water or grape soda."

"You have *grape* soda?" she asked, a note of amusement in her voice.

"What's wrong with that?"

"Nothing. It's just something my grandparents always drank."

"Well, your grandparents sound like they had excellent taste."

She laughed. "Okay, bring me a grape soda."

He headed into the kitchen and pulled two cans out of the fridge. Liking grape soda was actually a pain because restaurants rarely carried it, which was why he always had to stock it at home. But looking at the can now, with its generic clump of grapes, it did seem like a supremely un-manly drink. Maybe he should've offered her a shot of Jack or some Scotch. Only he didn't have any here, and he never drank much of either.

Brynn took the cold can from him with a smile. "Thanks."

He settled next to her on the blanket, popped the soda top, and reached for the remote. When he pushed play, the movie started up where he'd left off the other night, and he moved it back to the beginning.

"*Die Hard*?" Brynn glanced at him, the lights from the television glowing in her eyes. "How can it be the greatest movie of all time if it doesn't even have romance?"

"Oh, it's got romance."

Brynn pressed her lips together. "That's not what I've heard."

"Wait. You've never *seen* it?"

"Can't say that I have."

"Then you have to watch it." This was perfect. He got to see Brynn experience its greatness for the first time. He had all the background information, too, facts most people didn't know. "It's got everything. You'll see…"

She raised an eyebrow at him, and he leaned back right next to her, covering her hand with his. She took a swig of soda and then studied the can. "I don't know why more places don't have grape. It's actually really good."

"See? I'm right about the soda, so obviously I'm right about the movie."

"We'll see," she said. Then she leaned her head on his shoulder and he thought his heart might burst.

A few minutes in, he noticed she was watching him and not the movie. He looked down at her. "What?"

"Nothing. Sorry." She turned to face the TV and he did, too. But then his gaze drifted back to her and he couldn't look away. He liked watching other people's reactions to different scenes. But he especially liked watching her, every small smile or eyebrow twitch, and the way she jumped every time there was a loud noise.

Each time he'd grip her hand tighter, too, happy for the excuse.

And then he stopped paying attention to the movie and started plotting how he was going to kiss her at the end, no matter what.

. . .

Brynn glanced at Sawyer and found him looking back at her. Her pulse spiked and she was acutely aware of every place their skin touched. Earlier she'd been watching his expressions, noticing how into the movie he was. Seeing passion like that only made him that much more attractive, and it wasn't like he needed any help in that department.

She thought he might lean in for a kiss, and she wasn't sure if she was supposed to go for it or not… If this were strictly experimental—and it was—then science needed to know if kissing him again would be as good as it had been behind the stage, especially now that she was in control of the situation. It'd help her read the signs when she dated someone else. Yeah. That made total sense.

But she wasn't sure if she had played it cool long enough. Or was she reaching the prude, not-worth-his-time territory now? Was she supposed to kiss him, and then go back to cool and indifferent?

Holy crap, I'm totally going to screw this up. She looked down at the blanket they were sitting on and ran her hand across it, the wool texture rough under her skin. "You use this blanket for sleeping?"

Sawyer stared at her for a moment, probably wondering what had brought that about. Honestly, she was wondering the same thing. "Yeah...why?"

A voice in the back of her mind was shouting for her to stop, but her mouth kept on going anyway. "It looks like the type of blanket you'd use to ride a donkey."

One corner of his mouth twisted up. "You use blankets to ride donkeys? And how many donkeys have you ridden?"

He leaned in, so close now, the scent of his cologne invaded her senses. Her breath slowly leaked from her lungs, but none seemed to be coming in anymore. "No donkeys, actually. I'm just saying it looks like what you'd use if... I just think you should have something softer to cuddle up with."

He ran his knuckles down her arm and goose bumps broke out across her skin. "You look pretty soft."

She could feel every beat of her heart. *Thump, thump, thump.* "I'm warm, too."

She didn't know where it came from, but Sawyer's eyebrows jerked up and sweet satisfaction ran through her veins. She was actually doing this. Flirting. It was working, but now holding it all back made her feel like she might explode and possibly make a comment even stupider than the donkey-blanket one.

"Brynn…" He whispered her name into the air between them and her heart lurched. "I wish we weren't just friends, because I kinda want to kiss you now."

She smiled, leaning in the tiniest bit. "Just kinda?"

He slid his hand up her arm and behind her neck, his thumb resting at the rapidly beating pulse point under her jaw. "It's *all* I can think about. And since *Die Hard*'s currently on, that's saying something."

"You almost pulled off the romance, but then you had to go reference the action movie. I was hoping for a more poetic pickup line, coming from a writer and all."

He brushed his thumb over her skin, sending tingly heat in its wake. "Damn. So I blew it?"

She leaned closer. "I'm afraid so."

For a moment their breath mixed in the air between them, and then he brought his mouth down on hers. He started out gentle, his soft lips barely pressing against hers. Then the kisses grew in urgency, his tongue parting her lips and slipping into her mouth.

Intoxicating heat traveled through her, stealing away all the doubts she'd had earlier. When she pulled back, she was breathless and dizzy. She worried he'd push her for more, but he simply put his arm around her shoulders and curled her into him.

"This is the best part," he said as Bruce Willis confronted the bad guy. The rest was a lot of punching and shooting, and finally the credits rolled up the screen.

Brynn ran her hand across Sawyer's firm stomach. "I'm still waiting for the romance I was promised."

Sawyer gestured at the TV screen. "He got back together with his wife. Of course in the third movie, they're not together, but still… Romance."

Brynn lifted her head from his chest. "That's not even

close to romance! Love stories need to have the guy and the girl who meet, and then they realize they're perfect for each other, but of course the world's against them, so they have to fight for their love, so much so that they're willing to risk *everything* to be together."

Sawyer was looking at her like she was adorable, and she didn't want to be adorable. And—she realized way too late—she wasn't supposed to be so into romance, either.

"Uh, not that I believe in any of that stuff," she tried to cover. "But it makes a nice movie. Or a nice play. Story. Whatever. I know it's all fiction. I'm not saying—"

Sawyer kissed her again, a soft peck on the lips, but he lingered there and swept her hair behind her ear. "I'm glad you came over tonight."

"Yeah?"

She felt him smile. "Yeah. But just so you know, I can't let you slam *Die Hard*, romance or not. Make fun of my soda, blanket—whatever—but the movie's crossing a line."

She laughed. "Okay, I'll keep back my comments about how unlikely it was that any of that would occur. Not to mention how he just happens to—"

Sawyer put his finger to her lips.

Brynn laughed again and then pulled back enough so she could look Sawyer in the eyes. "Why do you love it so much, anyway? Not only that movie, but I'm guessing you're like that with all of them, since you write them. It's the way I get into plays. Even if I don't love it, I'm seeing the way they act it out and how they get into character. Movies are your plays."

He sighed and rolled so that his back was against the box, and she worried she'd said the wrong thing. She was asking too many questions. Acting too needy. Paul was right; she always screwed it up by talking too much.

"My dad had ALS," Sawyer said, running his palms down the legs of his jeans. "Most people know of it as Lou

Gehrig's disease."

From the *had*, she knew that he must've passed on. "I've heard of that, but I don't know what it means."

"It means his muscles started atrophying, and gradually they got worse and worse until he could hardly move." Sawyer turned his head toward her, casting half of it in shadows. "He was a carpenter and started having trouble at work—that was my sophomore year. After a while, it got to where he couldn't work anymore, then he could hardly even move. So he and I would watch movies together. Afterward, we'd sit and talk about them, argue about why they were good or bad, what worked and what didn't, and all the plot holes." He pointed his chin at the TV. "*Die Hard* was his favorite."

Brynn ran her fingers across her forehead. "Now I feel like a jerk for making fun of it."

Sawyer put his hand on her knee. "Don't. That's what we used to do after every movie. So one day I decided to write a screenplay, working in the things we liked and avoiding all the movie clichés that bothered us. I read it to him shortly before he died, and he told me it was good, even though it wasn't." He smiled, but there was so much sorrow behind it, and Brynn's heart ached for him. "So that's how I got into the movie biz. I decided I wouldn't stop until I wrote something that made it."

"And you did."

"Getting there, anyway." Sawyer glanced away and cleared his throat. "Sorry. Didn't mean to get into all that."

Brynn put her arms around his neck and kissed his cheek. He closed his eyes and let out an exhale. They sat like that for a moment, and then she noticed the time. She had to be up before the sun tomorrow. On top of that, Mondays were always hell days, filled with retired fishermen who were happy to get the lake back after the "too-busy weekend."

"I better go," she whispered. Then she pushed herself to

her feet. Sawyer stood, too, and walked with her across the living room.

When she turned to tell him good-bye, he grabbed her hand. "I'll walk you to your door."

"Oh, you don't need to."

"I know." His grip on her hand tightened. "But I'm going to."

Would it be cheesy to say the stars and moon were shining exceptionally brightly tonight? Or that the air, filled with the crisp smell that only living by the water brought, smelled extra delicious? Probably, so Brynn wouldn't say them aloud. Just hold them in until she could write them all down in her journal, so she'd never forget that for one night, at least, she'd felt the magic and butterflies, and everything she'd always dreamed of.

She unlocked her door, which swung open easily now, and turned to face Sawyer. Back in high school, she'd imagined he had some tragic past and kept his most intense thoughts buried under the surface, waiting to come out only for her. Maybe she hadn't been that far off.

Sawyer leaned down and kissed her, lingering long enough that her body heated and her breaths came faster and faster. "Good night, Brynn."

She managed a shaky good night in return. She moved to go inside, then whipped around. "Oh, I almost forgot. Regarding rehearsals. It's probably best if we act like nothing's going on between us. Not that I'm saying there's anything going on—"

"There's definitely something going on," he said with a smile that made heat pool low in her stomach.

Brynn licked her suddenly dry lips. The point was to make sure he didn't get the wrong idea, but now images were floating through her head that she needed to push away before she got herself into trouble. She'd definitely underestimated his effect on her. "I think it's best if we pretend nothing's changed."

"Okay. So you'll continue shooting me death glares, and I'll act like I'm not checking you out even though you're shooting me death glares. Got it."

"I do not...do that."

He nodded. "You do. More at first, but they still come out from time to time. What's that about, anyway?"

It's about the fact that you broke my heart once and you don't even remember. "Um, just the way you came in like you were all that."

"I'm not all that?" he asked in mock shock and hung his head. "That's so disappointing."

She couldn't help smiling. Again, she thought she'd misjudged how serious he was—in novels there was nothing like a hot broody guy, but in real life, she was a sucker for humor. Add both, and...yep, she was definitely in trouble. "Anyway... Like I was saying, it'll look bad if I start dating the director. I don't want to be one of *those* actresses. That's way too Hollywood for my tastes."

"But don't they sleep with the director to get the part? And you already have the part, though I'm not totally opposed to—"

She smacked his arm before he could finish, the tips of her ears growing hot. "Just...let's keep it on the down low, okay?"

"Whatever you want." He kissed her cheek and then moved his lips so close to her ear that they brushed it when he spoke. "But all bets are off the second rehearsals are over."

Then he simply turned around and left her alone, her legs wobbly and her heart pounding like a freight train.

Chapter Nine

The chilly morning air had Brynn gripping her warm mug of tea tightly and wishing for the sun to hurry up and clear the horizon. Dad was of the Early Worm Gets the Fish philosophy. It'd been a long time since she'd been willing to be on the lake at this ungodly hour, but when Dad had asked yesterday if she wanted to go fishing with him, she couldn't say no.

She spotted the familiar green and white boat. Dad was already there, vest and hat on, fishing pole in hand. He smiled at her as she approached. "Come on, we're burning daylight, and the fish are out there, just waiting to be caught."

"I think there'd have to *be* daylight for us to be burning any of it." Brynn stepped onto the boat, gripping the railing as it swayed. Dad handed her a fishing pole, already set with a spooner and a worm—she'd put plenty of worms on hooks before, but it was always nice when someone else did it for her.

Brynn perched on the seat up front and held on as Dad motored them away from shore. Water lapped the sides of the boat, rocking it in a way that made her want to close her eyes and fall asleep.

Last night she'd laid awake, residual butterflies in her stomach as she thought over her night with Sawyer. It all seemed like a dream. A delicious dream with kissing that made her want to take up making out with Sawyer as her new profession.

But in the harsh, almost-light of day, reality was setting in. She was lying to him—had been from almost the beginning. No more sugarcoating it. Hell, earlier yesterday, she'd been thinking of him as nothing more than a dating test run.

After that dinner with Carly she'd felt so vulnerable, though, and her feet walked her over to his place as though they had a mind of their own. She'd needed to feel wanted, and Sawyer had certainly done a good job of that.

Then he'd talked movies and opened up about his dad. She'd have to have an iron heart to not fall for him a little bit right then and there. But her emotions were having trouble figuring out the difference between real and fake. There was no denying that things between her and Sawyer were changing. Getting more intimate.

Getting out of control.

Dani had texted a couple nights ago, asking Brynn when she wanted to go out with Connor, the cop who might be the man of her dreams. What she should do was forget about Sawyer, get out her phone this second, and set it up. After lying to him, she didn't deserve to be with him for real, not the way she suddenly found herself wanting to be. It'd been a long time since the thought of seeing a guy again caused her so much anticipation she thought she might burst from it.

Was it so bad to ride it out a little longer? See what was there, if anything?

What if she went on a date with the other guy and it ruined everything that was starting with Sawyer?

Dad suddenly appeared next to her, making her realize that they'd stopped moving. He cast into the water and sat on the other seat. "It's been a while since I had company. It's nice."

He didn't usually talk much when they were out on the boat, but Brynn supposed it was nice to have someone there *in case* he wanted to say something. It was also the perfect segue for what she wanted to talk about…

Only now she was almost scared to ask. Her parents were one of those couples who'd stayed in love for decades, and Brynn needed to believe that kind of love could last forever. She took a sip of her lukewarm tea. "Mom doesn't come out much anymore, does she?"

Dad turned his reel slowly, never breaking the steady pace he'd perfected over the years. "She's busy."

Busy? Doing what? Coming into the shop and telling Brynn everything she was doing wrong, from dating to arranging lures? Apprehension squeezed her chest. "Is everything okay with you guys?"

Dad kept reeling, never taking his eyes off the end of his line. "We've both got time to do all the things we always wanted to. The hard part of running the shop was being surrounded by fishing equipment and never getting the chance to use it."

As she recalled, he'd spent most evenings on the water back then. Now he started his mornings there. How he could fish day in and day out and not tire of it, she had no idea. She did notice he didn't say that they were okay. But she didn't know how to ask the right questions, or if there were right questions. So she simply sat, watching the end of her pole. Unlike Dad, she didn't bother reeling. If a fish wanted the bait, he could do the work.

When the line tugged a couple minutes later, she knew she had something. She set the hook and then reeled it in. It was a tiny trout, barely longer than her hand.

Brynn removed the hook from the fish's lip. "I think you need to get bigger and a lot smarter, fishie. Next time, maybe you'll know better than a free breakfast that looks too good to be true." She tossed him back in and moved over to the tackle box to pull out the Power Bait. The paste apparently tasted like garlic and salmon eggs, but she liked it because it was glittery.

Dad stood, and she figured he was going to cast again, but then he sighed. "Your mom wants to pursue other interests. Says she's done the fishing thing long enough."

"There are other interests besides fishing?" Brynn joked.

He laughed. "Apparently. Waste of time, if you ask me."

She wanted to laugh, but he'd called her acting a waste of time before. Her parents used to think of theater as a cute hobby, one she'd eventually grow out of. They were more supportive now and went to every play; they seemed to finally get that she needed an outlet to keep her happy. Maybe Mom needed one now. "Other interests might not be all bad. She just needs to find something more interesting than my dating life."

"She worries about you. Paul, too. I thought once you were out of the house, she'd see you were okay, but she almost worries more." Dad cast again, the plunk in the water loud in the sudden silence. "She tells me I forced that store and the stress on you two. I know it's a big task."

"Honestly, I was worried about all the responsibility of running the shop at first, but it's more fun than I thought it'd be. It's what Paul and I want to do."

Dad's shoulders relaxed. "Well, I'm real proud of you two. It means a lot to me, and I'm sorry if I don't say it enough."

Somehow she'd forgotten that the only way to have a heart-to-heart with him was in the boat, hooks in the water. She set down her pole and hugged him, vowing to come out here more. "Thanks, Daddy."

He squeezed her back, and then reached into the cooler and handed her a juice box, just like he had when she was a little girl. She could see his lunch inside, too, which meant he'd be out here most of the day. Long after he dropped her back at the dock so she could go to work.

Out here all alone for hours, with only the fish for company. It seemed so sad, and for once, she got the feeling it wasn't exactly what he wanted, either.

Whatever was going on with him and Mom, Brynn prayed it would get fixed soon.

. . .

Sawyer pushed through the curtains on the stage and glanced around. He swore Brynn was purposely driving him crazy today, catching his eye and shooting him a smile that held a dozen secrets in it. Or maybe he just had a dirty mind.

"Brynn," he whispered. He heard voices and walked toward them. Brynn's hair was pulled up and she was in a very ruffled, very pink dress. The zipper in the back was only partway done, the fabric folded back, showing off a lot of skin.

His breathing grew shallow. He wondered if she'd accuse him of creeping around again. Right now, though, he didn't really care.

Aunt Wendy stepped into view and zipped up the dress, which was a buzz kill on multiple levels.

He went ahead and closed the distance, making his steps loud enough they'd hear him approach.

Brynn spun around to face him, then reached up and patted her bun. "Hey."

His aunt glanced at him, pins sticking out of her mouth. She stuck a couple into the waist of the dress, cinching it tighter. "Just finalizing the costumes," she mumbled, the sharp ends bobbing up and down and catching the light. "Luckily this one's already the right length, because there's way too much lace and ruffles to try to match."

Brynn smoothed a hand down the skirt. "Could you imagine wearing these kinds of clothes every day? I used to wish I could, but they're definitely not very comfortable."

"Well, before now, I'd never guess they could look so good."

Brynn's cheeks colored as she glanced down, and he wanted to throw her over his shoulder and carry her out of there.

"Did you need something?" Aunt Wendy asked.

"No, just…heard voices." He didn't want to leave, so he moved over to a chair and sat down. "I figure I might as well learn everything I can about putting on plays while I'm here." Actually, he was glad Aunt Wendy had talked him into the play. Especially *this* play. *The Importance of Being Earnest* had a ton of great lines—and it didn't hurt that Brynn had a natural ability to deliver them in a way that was going to have the audience eating out of her hand. That Leo guy could use some work, but maybe Sawyer only felt that way because he didn't like seeing him fawn over Brynn, acting or not.

But the entire plot was so well done. Two guys lying about being named Earnest to get the women who claimed they would only love someone by that name. The lies get messier and funnier with each scene. But that finale, when Jack's true identity is discovered and the person he never knew he was happens to satisfy both Gwendolyn *and* her disapproving mother, was pure genius. Sawyer had spent the past few weeks analyzing how Oscar Wilde had pulled it off so perfectly, and he'd even started reading his other works, studying them to try to make his own writing better.

"The costume part isn't very exciting," Aunt Wendy said. "I'm only making alterations."

Sawyer kept his eyes on Brynn's. "That's okay. I'll just sit here and soak it all in."

His aunt stood and stepped back, running her gaze up and down Brynn. Sawyer couldn't help but do the same, even though it was for an entirely different reason. The whole get-up screamed innocence in a way that made him want to be the one who showed her the dark side.

Brynn raised her eyebrows like she could read his mind.

Aunt Wendy gave one sharp nod. "Yes, I think it'll work. Stay like that for a few more minutes if you don't mind. I've got a slip in the car that goes under the skirt to give it a little more volume, and I want to make sure it works with the dress."

Perfect. A few minutes alone in the costume room with Brynn.

"Sawyer? There's a fake tree crammed in my car, too. Can you come help me bring it in?"

"Suuure." He reluctantly followed her out. Once she got to the steps of the stage, though, he patted his pockets. "I think I dropped my keys. I'm gonna go grab them before they end up lost in a sea of costumes and props. You go ahead, and I'll be right behind you."

It sounded lame, even to him, but if his aunt suspected he was lying, she didn't say anything. He rushed backstage and charged into the room where Brynn was. Her eyes widened, and he took a couple of large steps to get to her. His mouth collided with hers with more force than he meant to, but she took it in stride, wrapping her arms around his neck and moving her lips with his.

He flinched when a stray pin pricked his finger, but the sensation of Brynn's lips on his dulled it enough that he didn't care. "I've been wanting to do that all day."

"Practice did seem torturously long with you sitting there just out of reach." She smiled and kissed him again, sucking lightly on his bottom lip. "This feels very making-out-in-the-janitor's-closet-at-school."

He kissed her neck. "Did you do a lot of that in high school?"

She gave a sputtery laugh. "Oh yeah, that was me."

"I bet all the guys were after you." She tensed, and he pulled back to look at her face. "What?"

"Nothing," she said, but she was stepping away.

"What's up? Why are you being weird now?"

Brynn crossed her arms. "Maybe I'm weird every day. Is something wrong with that?"

Sawyer lowered his eyebrows. He knew he was approaching dangerous territory. In the back of his mind, a voice whispered that this was why he should stay away from actresses. But he wasn't sure if he could stay away from *this* actress anymore, not after last night. Not when he knew what it was like to open up to her like he never could with anyone else. To hold her in his arms and kiss her.

"Look, I just want to be honest with you." She winced as if those words hurt her.

He tensed, waiting for the blow. With every second she didn't speak, the knot in his stomach got tighter. He barely knew the girl. Surely nothing she said could be *that* bad.

"It's just that..." She glanced away, and then her gaze came back to him. She let out a long breath. "Anyone could walk in at any time. My reputation in the community theater is important, and Wendy could come back any minute. And by the way, weren't you supposed to be helping her?"

Damn it. He'd gotten carried away and forgot his aunt was waiting for him. "Yeah. I'll be right back." He started toward the door and then turned around. "Hey, don't worry. I get it. No kissing in the theater."

"Thanks." One corner of her mouth twisted up. "And now I'm thanking you for not kissing me." Her eyes met his, an emotion he couldn't name in them that didn't quite match the amusement in her voice.

"Yeah, kinda adds to that complex you're set on giving me."

Brynn gave a casual shrug. "And here I thought I was being subtle about trying to take your ego down a few notches."

Now they were joking again, the tension leaked from his body, and all he could think about was kissing her. If that wasn't a possibility at the theater, the solution was to get her out of here as soon as possible. "After this, I have to go pick up a few things for the house. I was thinking... It'd be nice to have help choosing fixtures and paint. Make sure everything matches and that kind of thing. If you wouldn't mind."

Wow. Not only was he babbling, but he was also asking her to go pick out home improvement supplies with him. It was a sorry excuse for a date, not to mention something one would do with someone he was moving in with. All he knew was he needed to pick up supplies while he was in Charlotte, and he didn't want to wait until tomorrow after rehearsal to see Brynn again.

"Sure." She shot him a grin that had his mind back in the gutter. "But you'll owe me."

Wanting to get this part of the evening over with, Sawyer hurried outside, where Aunt Wendy was still digging items out of her car.

"I'm glad you're enjoying the play," she said. "I knew you'd get into it if you gave it a chance." She turned to him, a giant hat with lots of pink flowers in her hand and a garment bag hanging over her other arm. "See, there's culture here, same as New York. You can find plenty of inspiration, plus life goes at a slower pace."

Sawyer suspected Mom had enlisted his aunt's help talking him into staying. "It is nice here, and it's definitely more relaxed…" He was going to start with the *but*s, *but* he figured it wouldn't matter. Wendy would keep listing reasons to stay, and he didn't want to argue with her, the way he had with Mom yesterday morning.

Come to think of it, though, maybe he should stick around just a little longer. Another couple of weeks wouldn't kill him. It'd make Mom happy.

He told himself that the thought had nothing to do with a certain girl next door.

Chapter Ten

"See," Brynn said, shooting Sawyer a big smile that lit up her eyes. He was too busy looking at her to see. She had her dark hair piled in a bun and several strands had come loose around her face. He'd never thought of a woman's neck as sexy before, but Brynn had a sexy neck. A sexy everything, really.

She stuck her fist on her hip. "Are you even paying attention?"

He finished tearing the plastic off the new paint roller and set it on the recently finished granite-topped counter. "I'm paying attention, just not to the paint."

A flush spread up the neck he'd been admiring, into her cheeks, and happiness radiated through his chest. He'd spent the last week watching Brynn on the stage, counting down to the moment when he could call rehearsal and be alone with her. She made the most random yet charming comments and was completely unlike any girl he'd ever dated. There were still times he'd say something that would make her intoxicating smile fade from her face. As hard as he tried, he couldn't pinpoint exactly what it was. And every time he asked, she just said, "Nothing," and proceeded to pull away.

But now she was here in his house, ready to help him paint, and everything felt right with the world. He walked over to her, slipped his arms around her waist, and kissed her. Her soft lips opened under his, and he considered telling her to forget about painting.

She pulled back a couple of inches and tilted her head toward the wall. "Tell me I was right."

He took in the chocolate-milk-colored section of paint, and how it looked next to the espresso wood cabinets and the pale hardwood floors. When he'd asked for her help picking paint colors and that was what she'd chosen, he didn't know if it was going to go together. But he'd gotten the paint anyway, because, well, she seemed so excited about it.

He twisted her so that her back was against his chest and tucked his head on her shoulder. "You were right." He wasn't just saying it, either. "It ties in the cabinets and floor and gives the whole room a warm feel."

"It makes me think that when you get settled in, you should bake me something chocolate in your kitchen." She nudged him with her elbow. "Hint, hint."

He smiled, but then it hit him. He'd mentioned the possibility of going to California, but he'd never clarified his stay here was only temporary, had he? That this wasn't his house, and his life was somewhere else.

He should tell her.

"So…" She spun around and bounced on the balls of her feet. "Does that mean I've got the green light to keep going?"

He tapped her nose. "Go crazy."

She gave him a kiss on the cheek that was more attack than kiss, a quick smash of her lips that made him laugh, and then poured more of the pale brown paint into the tray and picked up the roller brush. He took the other and they stood side by side, the breeze off the lake blowing in through the open doors of the patio.

Brynn started humming, and he wondered if she even knew she was doing it.

Sawyer stretched to reach the spot near the top. "Usually I don't get to see you in the day. You're even perkier than at night, and I didn't know that was possible." Yes, she was beyond perky this morning, but he was also fishing for information. He'd tried to get her to do things with him during the day before, but she always said she couldn't and then quickly changed the subject.

She grinned at him. "I like painting. Seeing the transformation. Plus, I know this makes me sound like I huff paint, but it smells good to me. The excitement usually wears off about halfway through a project, though, so now you're warned."

He gave an exaggerated gasp. "You'd quit on me?"

"Depends on what I get if I finish." She winked at him and his throat went dry. Then, as usual, she looked away. That was what amused him most about when she delivered a line like that—she seemed as surprised by it as he did. And he liked to take advantage of that by saying something bold in return and watching her eyes widen or her cheeks redden.

He moved right up behind her and leaned his lips next to her ear. "I have a few ideas."

She shivered against him and if he didn't rein it in, she was going to be feeling exactly what he was thinking about.

Her arm slowed as she brought the roller down the wall. He was still holding one in his right hand, trying to keep it away from her so he didn't completely ruin her clothes.

"Sawyer…" Her voice came out breathless, and it completely unraveled him. Did she have any idea what she did to him? She was like a drug—once he had a taste he wanted more. This girl had knocked down all his usual barriers in a matter of weeks, and he didn't care. He *wanted* to let her all the way in.

Shit. No, not all the way. I can't... He thought of his mom drained after a day of taking care of his dad. Panic was rising up, digging its claws into his lungs.

"You need some air? I need some air." He dropped his roller into the paint tray and headed out the back door, his heart beating against his rib cage like it was trying to make an escape.

· · ·

Brynn wasn't sure what had just happened. Sawyer was flirting—and then some. Over the past few days she'd tried to keep up her guard, pulling away when things got serious, trying to find that balance. As happy as she was whenever she was with him, there was always that twinge of guilt. The reminder that he liked her for the wrong reasons. Brynn was starting to put on a show so much that fiction was slowly bleeding into reality.

She'd thought about confessing the truth almost every time they were together. But when she'd told Paul she was thinking of coming clean and telling Sawyer how glad she was he'd moved back, her brother said she was so close to hooking him, and not to screw it up now.

A pit formed in her stomach. *Maybe I already screwed it up.*

She tried to remember if she'd said anything that might scare him off. She hadn't quoted any plays or books.

Then it hit her. *The kitchen. I said I wanted him to bake for me. That sounds like I'm trying to domesticate him or something. But that was a few conversations ago...*

Maybe it was the paint huffing comment. You're not supposed to tell people that you like smelling paint. She was sure that wasn't it either, though.

Determined to fix…whatever it was, she stepped onto the back porch. Her house had a tiny window that overlooked the lake, but she rarely went into the backyard. The lady who'd lived there before her had landscaped with rocks and ceramic geese and gnomes and left no place to really sit. Basically, it was where lawn ornaments went to die. Brynn had moved the boy and girl gnomes closer so it looked like they were kissing, but she was only renting the place and couldn't do much more.

But the large, raised deck of this house had a prime view of the glittering lake, tiny boats leaving white trails across the water, and birds flying through the cottony clouds and unbelievably blue sky. Even though she'd grown up fishing on that lake, its picture-perfect beauty still struck her when she took the time to stand and take it in.

And maybe she was avoiding talking to Sawyer the tiniest bit. Somewhere along the way this relationship stopped being a practice run and started being real, and her heart ached at the thought of whatever was happening between them ending. If she were being honest with herself, she'd wanted it to be more from the beginning, regardless of their past that only she remembered.

She took another step and he glanced back at her, devastatingly handsome as always. She took in a deep breath and said, "Hey," hoping it was enough, because she didn't know what else to say.

He stared at her for a moment—or maybe it was for three years. It certainly felt like that long. Then he held out his hand to her. She clasped it, the calluses he'd most likely gotten working on the house rough against her skin. With his other hand, he brushed away the hair the breeze was sending across her face and rested his palm on her cheek.

She wasn't sure what he was feeling or thinking, but the

mixture of panic at this potentially ending and the pleasure of his touch had her thinking she was already past the point of no return.

"I think you're amazing," he said.

Her hands started shaking and she clenched them into fists. This was the classic break-up speech. It'd been used on her before, and she'd used it once herself.

"But I should also tell you…" Sawyer glanced down at the deck. "I'm not big on commitment. Actually, I run from it."

Everything inside her turned cold and hard. Ice formed over her heart; her lungs stopped expanding. *You always knew this would happen, you idiot. What, you thought he'd actually fall for you?*

It was like that moment in high school when he'd crushed her all over again. Only this was worse because she actually knew him now, knew he was one of the rare, hard-to-find good guys. Or so she'd thought.

She started to pull away, but he tightened his grip on her, keeping her next to him. "I didn't say anything about commitment," she said. She'd been so careful not to. "If this is about me telling you to bake for me, that was a joke."

"It's not. I'm not saying…" He blew out a breath. "If I were going to stay here, then maybe… But I'm only here for another week, two at most. The house is almost finished, and once it and the play are done, I've got to go back to my real life. I know I should've said something earlier, but I didn't think it'd turn into…this." And what was *this*? Was he saying he wanted more? Or that he could tell she did?

"I'm just trying to be honest," he said.

Lately she'd decided honesty was overrated. She could've gone without knowing this for a few more days. Weeks. Forever.

He's leaving. That thought spun around and around in

her head, opening up a hollow emptiness in her chest. Sawyer no longer in town. Not in the beautiful house next door he was pouring his heart and soul into. It was so…wrong.

But apparently this wasn't his *real life*—he'd said it like staying in North Carolina would be ridiculous. As hypocritical as it was, considering she currently wasn't exactly living her real life either, that made her want to shake him. This place was her home. And he belonged here, too; couldn't he see that?

Or maybe she was the one who couldn't see right. *I don't know him. Not really.* It took more than a few stolen backstage kisses and some stories about his father to know him. Obviously.

And to think she'd even considered coming clean. There was really no point now, was there?

Sawyer brushed his thumb across the top of her cheek. "Say something."

The sinking sensation in her gut grew. "That's totally fine. I mean, it's not like I thought this was anything serious. And I don't even know how long I'll stick around here, either." She didn't know where that came from. The world was spinning and her thoughts were hard to catch hold of.

"Are you thinking about going back to LA?"

What she wouldn't do to go back in time and undo that lie. It was far too late to fix it now, but guilt still filled the empty void in her stomach. "I don't know."

Too many emotions were nearing the surface, tears were rising, and she'd simply die if she cried in front of him. That'd probably scare him off for good. Then again, maybe that would be a good thing. She forced the corners of her mouth to lift into a smile. "You know, I just remembered I have something I need to do before rehearsal. So I'll see you then."

Sawyer caught her wrist. "Brynn."

She tugged away from him and rushed through the living

room and out the front door. It was the first time all week they hadn't kissed good-bye. Her lips and her body—and her heart—already missed it.

. . .

Sawyer watched Brynn walk away, heard the door close behind her, and hung his head. He'd really screwed it up this time. But it was better for her to know now, right? Better for him, too. A few days ago he'd been thinking about sticking around longer for her, but that'd only make it worse in the end. Now they both knew there was an expiration date. Maybe this would save them from the kind of messy breakup that included dish-throwing or left emotional scars.

With that mantra in his mind, he headed back into the kitchen, picked up his roller, and got back to work. He missed Brynn's humming. Watching her as she painted. Her calming presence. Her absence took up all the space in the room, glaring at him in every place he tried to look. In the matter of thirty minutes, he'd gone from having the best day ever to one of the worst.

He told himself he'd done the right thing.

If only it didn't feel so wrong.

Chapter Eleven

Since this morning hadn't been bad enough, Brynn had to drive all the way to the Bait and Tackle without having tea first. She'd meant to pick some up yesterday, but she'd been too busy riding an emotional roller coaster.

"Morning," Paul said with a smile, and she wanted to punch him in the face—he was way too happy and bright-eyed this early. She zombie shuffled past him, squinting against the bright lights, and walked into the office.

"You hungover or somethin'?" Paul asked, way too loud.

Yeah, love hungover. "Or somethin'," she answered, reaching for the coffee Paul kept brewing until about noon. The mugs didn't look very clean, but she was so desperate for caffeine she picked one up anyway. She gave it a halfhearted wipe with one of the brown paper towels she always felt did a better job removing a layer of skin than drying hands, and filled the mug with coffee.

She frowned at the lack of cream and sugar. How could Paul drink this stuff black? She shuddered at the first sip, but eventually her tongue was burned enough she didn't have to taste it anymore.

"I don't think I've seen you grumpy since high school," he said with a note of amusement, that stupid smile still on his face.

"So glad my grumpiness causes you joy." She moved out by the register and set her mug down on the counter. "Hey, have you gone fishing with Dad at all this week?"

"Haven't had time. He came in for a few minutes yesterday afternoon, though."

"How did he seem?"

Paul shrugged. "Like Dad. We talked fishing, sales numbers. The usual."

Brynn heard the chime over the door and groaned. She didn't want to deal with people today.

Paul tapped the counter in front of her. "I've got it. Take a few minutes and listen to show tunes or do whatever it is you do to make yourself so bubbly all the time."

Brynn ducked into the office, sat in the swivel chair, and propped her head in her hands. Show tunes weren't going to help her now. Not after what happened at the end of last night's rehearsal.

She'd tried to be cool after Sawyer's whole bomb about running from commitment and how he was leaving...but she'd failed miserably—more like completely lost it. And now she wondered if Sawyer would ever talk to her again.

I wasn't that bad, was I? A tight knot formed in her stomach. *Yes, yes I was.*

The entire rehearsal had been torture, to say the least. Every time her gaze had drifted to Sawyer, her heart would tug. And the times his eyes met hers sent squeezing pain through her lungs. She'd missed cues and lines, and by the end of it, all the other actors were as exasperated as she was.

When everyone had filtered off the stage, she wasn't sure whether to bolt or stay. Talking to Sawyer would be painful; not talking to him would be painful. She'd waited too long to decide, though, because he'd walked toward her, a determined set to his jaw. He stopped right in front of her and the air shifted, heavy and pressing against her skin like a wool blanket.

"I've felt like shit all afternoon," he'd said.

And she'd thought, *Good, at least I'm not alone in the shitiness feeling.* She'd opened her mouth to try to say something, but then pressed her lips together, not trusting her words to come out steady. Then she'd told herself to rein it in. Stay in character. Jaded. Strong. Not interested in a relationship, anyway.

Sawyer rubbed the back of his neck. "I finished painting the kitchen and it looks good." He'd taken a hesitant step closer. "Wanna come over and see it?"

"I can't," she said, which was true, because it'd be too hard for her to keep up the act for that long. "I've got an early morning tomorrow." Also true, but before his earlier confession, she would've gone over anyway.

"Brynn." He'd put his hand on her shoulder and squeezed. Her throat ached from holding back her emotions.

She hadn't been able to look him in the eye, so she'd focused on the fake tree behind him. "It's not because of what you told me earlier, I swear. In fact, that works out perfectly for me. My friend's been talking about setting me up with this guy forever, and now I can tell her to go ahead without feeling bad."

"Okay. Well, maybe you can come over tomorrow night."

"Actually, I'm going to be really busy during the next few days."

"Doing what?"

She'd pulled away far enough that his hand dropped. "I have a job. What, you think I'm just a spoiled California girl whose daddy pays for everything?"

"Of course not. I never said anything like that."

Irritation had bubbled up, and suddenly, she was pissed. At him for making her like him so much, and at herself for letting it happen when she knew better. The anger had eclipsed the pain nicely and helped her work up the indifference she was going for. "I'll catch you later." She'd started past him, but he stepped into her path.

"So, where do you work?"

Did he not get that she was trying to make a dramatic exit? She'd blown out her breath. "At a shop."

"Which shop?"

She glanced up, meeting his eyes, trying to ignore the way her heart lurched. "Does it matter?"

If he said yes, she wasn't sure how she'd respond. Since she'd acted like she'd never fished before when he took her, she'd feel pretty stupid admitting she worked at a bait shop. And if he came into Bigfish, there would be complications with Paul, and the less Sawyer inserted himself into her life, the better. That way, it would be easier when he left.

A sharp pain had pierced the center of her chest.

"I guess not," Sawyer said. "Unless you want me to come in and visit sometime?" Hope had flickered in his eyes and the pain spread through her lungs.

"No thanks. I've got enough men who only want one thing visiting me already." With that, she'd left, her exit even more dramatic than she'd wanted.

Now, Brynn dropped her head on the desk and let herself wallow in the awful, nauseous feeling she'd had ever since. She'd meant fishing equipment—well, that'd been what she was thinking, but she knew how it'd sound. After she'd gotten home, she'd watched out the window, waiting for the light to go on next door, hoping she might gather up the courage to apologize.

After a while she'd given up and gone to bed. But she

hadn't fallen asleep.

"Hey, sis, maybe you could get out here and help me?" Paul's voice was extra sugary, so he must be dealing with a lot of customers, and they must be in near proximity. When she came out of the office, the nasty coffee she'd consumed churning in her gut, making her even sicker, she saw there were several customers. Including Howard, the guy who came in to grin and ogle her while he bought fishing equipment.

Thanks for that, karma.

"So, what's up with you today?" Paul asked when they hit a lull. Then his eyebrows shot up. "Oh no, you messed it up with that guy, didn't you? I told you to hold back. What did you do? Take him to your place and show him all your kissing statues?"

Brynn shoved him. "Thanks for being so damn sensitive. And no, I didn't show him my statues. It's not like I have a ton; there are only a few."

"Enough for most guys to see them and run for the hills. Not to mention that painting in your living room."

The urge to punch her brother in the face was back. "It's a famous work of art. Pardon the hell out of me for being cultured."

"Oh yeah, what's that work of art called?" A smirk quirked his lips.

He knew it was *The Kiss* by Gustav Klimt, a beautiful painting with colors and flowers and a man kissing a woman on the cheek. Just like he knew she'd gotten it for Christmas when she was fifteen. He'd also mocked her endlessly for it then.

"It doesn't matter," she said, trying to convince herself as she said it. "That guy was a fill-in. Practice. Dani's going to set me up with someone who's more my type, and now I know what not to do."

What she would be doing was guarding her heart, because putting it out there to get stomped on totally sucked. The chime announced a new customer, only it wasn't any regular old customer. Carly Johnson came into the store wearing the tiniest shorts known to man and gave Paul a huge grin, displaying every one of her blindingly white teeth.

"Hey, baby." She threw her arms around Paul and kissed him.

Oh, sure, mock a painting for having a cheek kiss and then swap spit in your place of business.

Not bothering to untwine himself from his new girlfriend, Paul glanced back at Brynn. "Hey, you know how you had yesterday off?"

Warning bells rang out like mad. "You mean how I actually took a whole day off instead of coming in to work for half a day when I'm *supposed* to have a full day?"

"Carly and I are going to sneak out for lunch," he said, ignoring her question. "I'll be back in an hour and a half, two tops."

Brynn might've been able to say no if he hadn't flashed her a goofy grin. Stupid jerk brother and her desire for him to be happy. "You owe me. And I need you to get that box down first. I could reach it if I have to but—"

"No worries, I got it." Paul patted Carly on the butt and then headed to the back.

Carly smiled and stared at Brynn for so long that she wondered if the girl was part robot and didn't need to blink. Finally, Carly rebooted and sprang into motion. "I know I said it the other night, but I'm really glad we have the chance to get to know each other better. I just adore Paul."

"That's nice."

"Yeah, I've dated so many losers in my life. Finally, I was

like, no more! I put it out to the universe that I wanted a kind man who'd treat me right, and then I met Paul." She sighed, a dreamlike expression on her face.

Wow. Who put fairy dust in your Cheerios this morning?

A thought hit Brynn. Warning bells went off again—actually this was more like three-alarm-fire level. She shouldn't ask. Knew it would come back to bite her somehow, because apparently Carly was more in touch with the universe than she was.

"So, you, uh, dated Sawyer Raines in high school, right? He was pretty hot." She felt like an idiot admitting it aloud, regardless of the fact that it was, indeed, a fact. "Seemed like a nice guy, too, but I didn't know him very well."

"Sawyer Raines. Yeah, he was definitely hot." Carly lifted herself onto the counter, crossing one toned, tan leg over the other. "He was one of my better boyfriends, which is sad since he ignored me half the time. Then he went all weird and wouldn't answer my calls or talk to me. It was like dating a post. I kind of just blew up that day in the cafeteria, you know?"

Brynn nodded, though she really didn't know.

"I shouldn't have dumped him like that." Carly's eyes widened. "Oh, if you're thinking I'd ever do that to Paul, I wouldn't."

"That's…not why I asked. You know what, never mind."

"I actually heard he was in town again."

"I had no idea," Brynn said. What was one more lie, when you were already drowning in all your others?

• • •

Sawyer had been staring at the blinking cursor for about an hour. He'd written a few sentences between the three cups of coffee, but he ended up deleting them. He hadn't risked going to the lake house this morning, justifying that the paint needed time to dry anyway. Even though what it probably needed was a second coat.

He put his fingers on his keyboard and started typing.

As she painted, he watched her side profile, the way her mouth would quirk up at the corner, and how her shirt inched up every time she rolled above her head, showing off a strip of pale skin he wanted to get his hands on... And then the coolest girl he'd ever dated walked out of his life for good.

Well, she hadn't exactly walked out of his life for good. He'd seen her a few hours later. But that hadn't gone so great either. Suddenly he was picturing his heroine as Brynn and himself as the hero, and he wanted to add in racy scenes he didn't normally write.

He deleted the sentences he'd just written—which were more in novel form than screenwriting form anyway, not to mention that they sounded like a sappy romance. He closed his laptop and scrubbed a hand across his face.

Everything had gotten so messed up yesterday. It didn't help that he had to sneak around backstage, hiding the fact that he needed to talk to Brynn alone. When he finally caught up to her, she'd thrown out that bit about how nice it was that she could go out with another guy. Like he wasn't aware that she had plenty of options besides him. It was something Zoey would do—try to make him jealous.

This was what he got for attempting to date an actress. One he was directing, no less, which only made everything more entwined and complicated.

I never learn.

That was unfair to Brynn, though. She was different from Zoey in every way. Sweet and funny, always looking at the world through rose-colored lenses. Once in a while he'd even heard her whispering lines under her breath, smiling the same way she would onstage, almost like she couldn't help but be lost in whatever world she'd escaped to.

She got excited over paint and fancy cabinet handles, for God's sake. He remembered stumbling across her backstage all those weeks ago, singing at the top of her lungs.

Being around her felt like standing next to the sun. Except now he was in the dark again, and he hated it.

It didn't help that none of the plot points in his screenplay were coming together like they needed to. Between the pressure to make it live up to the first, and his inability to stop thinking about Brynn, he was completely stuck.

Sawyer shoved his laptop in his bag and stood. He needed to walk around for a bit. Maybe visit a few shops—or all of them—until he found Brynn. There weren't *that* many in this town, right?

The comment she'd made yesterday had him picturing her as a Hooters waitress. He didn't like that thought at all, guys going in to check her out and hit on her. But he'd be lying if he said he wasn't a *little* interested in seeing Brynn in that uniform.

She does not *work at Hooters. What's wrong with you, Raines?*

He'd see Brynn tonight onstage anyway. Even if she didn't talk to him. So he decided to stick with his plan of walking and getting air, hoping it'd provide inspiration.

A few minutes into his walk, his phone buzzed. Speak of the devil. Zoey hadn't tried to call him in a while—probably because he never answered—and he deleted the voice mails unheard. She might not know that, but she obviously knew he wasn't going to answer. So she texted, the one way he'd be sure to see part of the message simply by glancing at his phone's display.

I really need to talk. I'm so sorry, and I know I don't deserve it, but please call me.

Sawyer shook his head. He was starting to wonder if he should change his number.

This was what commitment got you: a psycho ex who wouldn't leave you alone. They hadn't spoken since her lies had blown up in her face, and after what she did, she definitely didn't deserve anything from him.

He pocketed his phone. Maybe it was good that things with Brynn had turned out like this. He'd just finish the house, get the play done, and then he'd move to California and start fresh.

The more he thought about it, the more he decided that was the right decision for him. A new adventure. Focusing solely on his career. Forgetting about all women. For a while, anyway...

But then dark hair caught his eye. She was a few paces ahead of him, walking next to a girl with bronze skin that contrasted with Brynn's pale tone. And it was definitely Brynn—he could tell by the way she walked, and how she was swinging her arms all around, the way she did when she talked about something she was really in to.

He should probably turn the other way and go back to the coffee shop. But now he was curious. Besides, he was walking here before he saw her. Not like he was stalking her or anything, though he might've if she would've told him where she worked.

Brynn's laugh carried back to him, and while he'd been telling himself he didn't need the drama the female species brought, he wanted to see her eyes light up with that laugh.

He wanted to be the one making her laugh.

While he definitely wasn't opposed to taking things further than kissing, that wasn't the only reason he wanted to spend time with her. Even if they only hung out for the next few weeks, it'd be enough. He just wasn't ready to let her go yet.

He quickened his pace. When he got right behind her, he said, "Fancy meeting you here."

She spun around so fast he almost barreled right into her. "What are you doing here?" Her eyes darted around as if she'd been caught in the middle of a bank heist.

"I was writing at the coffee shop"—he gestured toward it—"but I was stuck, so I decided to walk for a bit. Clear out my thoughts and try again. Then I saw you, so…" Now he was thinking he should've walked the other way. Brynn didn't look happy to see him. In fact, she looked tired. Pretty, but tired.

He'd had a hard time sleeping last night, so he probably looked about the same. He thought the perfect way to solve that problem was to take her back home and cuddle up with her for a while.

"I'm Dani," the other girl said when the silence had stretched far past the awkward level. She smiled at him. "Sawyer, I presume."

"Not that I was talking about you," Brynn said, sweeping her hair off her face. "I mean, I was, but only because of the play and you're the director. Not because—"

Sawyer stepped forward and kissed her. She gasped into his mouth, and he put his hands on either side of her face, soaking in the moment in case it was the last time he got to kiss her.

She sagged against him, parting her lips and letting him kiss her deeper. Then she broke the kiss and, running a hand down her hair, she glanced at Dani.

"Well, I'll let you ladies get back to your day. Brynn, see you tonight." He walked past her, his heart beating wildly in his chest, and his libido way too fired up to be around so many people.

There. Let the other guy try to top that.

. . .

Brynn put her fingers over her lips and looked at Dani. "That was...unexpected." Here she was judging her brother and Carly for kissing in the store, and she'd just done the same thing with Sawyer, only with a lot more people around.

Dani smiled. "It was pretty hot, actually. The boy knows what he wants, and it's *you*."

Happiness and sorrow battled it out for a moment before sorrow won. "But he only wants me for a few weeks." She couldn't deny that kiss had taken her breath away. It was one of those romantic kisses she'd always dreamed of, where the guy didn't care who was around or what else was going on.

Dani continued down the sidewalk, toward the ice cream shop they'd been headed to before they ran into Sawyer. "You never know what a difference a few weeks makes. I'm not saying he'll change his mind, but you've been talking about him since I came into the shop today, and I can tell you like him. Otherwise you wouldn't have postponed going out with Connor."

Brynn had planned on asking about the supposed hottie police officer as soon as Dani showed up, but she'd launched into her frustration over Sawyer first. And now she wasn't sure if she should go through with it. "I do like him. But he... doesn't really know who I am." Brynn confessed it all, from what had happened with him in high school until now, and the mess of lies she'd gotten herself into. "I'm afraid if he found out who I really was, he wouldn't like me anymore. And what does it matter if he's just gonna leave?"

Dani pressed her lips together. "You're going to have to decide how much of yourself to put out there. But I'm not sure it's such a good idea to pretend to be a different person. As someone who's pulled off a scheme, I can tell you, it always ends up messy."

"Yeah, but your scheme got you Wes. Would you really go back and change it?"

Dani glanced down at the diamond on her finger and smiled. "Good point. But as your friend, who likes you the way you are, I think you should be yourself."

"I'll be myself," Brynn said. "Just a better version of myself." She lowered her voice. "And seriously, I've never felt the way I do with him. I actually feel confident and pretty and the chemistry... No one's ever taken my breath away with a kiss like that. It'd be a shame to give it up, right? Better to have loved and lost than never to have loved at all?"

Dani shrugged. "I guess so. But be careful."

"I will. Now, what did you need to talk to me about? I've totally hijacked this ice cream trip."

As they got their dessert, Dani explained that Wes had a bunch of groomsmen, and when she only had his sisters and her college roommate, her mother-in-law told her she needed one more to make it even. Dani licked chocolate syrup off her spoon. "I don't know why evenness matters, but when they asked if there was anyone else I'd want to be in my wedding party, I thought of you..."

Realization hit Brynn. "You're asking me to be a bridesmaid?"

"If you want to be. I know it'll probably be kinda lame, just a lot of standing in a pretty dress."

"That sounds awesome to me!" Brynn leaned over the table and hugged Dani.

"Well, this went better than expected," Dani said with a laugh. "If I were you, I would've asked for more than ice cream in exchange."

As Dani went over details for the wedding—and even

pulled out a bridal magazine—Brynn couldn't help but think about how she wanted that one day. Having off-the-charts chemistry with Sawyer was amazing, but an annoying voice was whispering it'd never be enough for her. That she'd never be able to relax knowing they not only wanted different things from a relationship, but also he had fallen for the glamorous, flippant actress she was only pretending to be.

She longed to look across at a guy whom she loved and know he wanted to spend his life with her, too, and there was no way that was where she and Sawyer were headed.

Maybe her life was doomed to be a love-free tragedy forever.

Chapter Twelve

When Brynn pulled into the back parking lot, Sawyer's car was there and he was standing next to it. The sight of him was enough to make her stomach swirl with anticipation. Her brain apparently didn't get the message that she was still deciding what to do about her director dilemma.

She'd almost texted Dani twice this afternoon, telling her to set up a date with the cop. It was always good to have options. But then she'd think of how she'd feel if Sawyer went out with someone else, and guilt would weigh her down.

She got out of the car, her heart beating faster every second. "Hey."

"I figured we should clear the air before practice so we don't have the kind of rehearsal we had yesterday," Sawyer said.

"Probably a good plan." She didn't know what to do with her hands.

"Also figured if you were mad that I kissed you today, you'd just hit me with your car." He cracked a smile.

The knot in her stomach loosened as she smiled back. "If

I didn't have that warrant out for my arrest already, I might consider it."

See, things were easy between them. Maybe it was all the practice, but flirting came more naturally. She even let some of her real self slip through without making a fool of herself.

He took a step toward her, and she reciprocated. One more step and he wrapped his arms around her waist. He buried his head in her neck, his breath warm against her skin. Then he kissed his way up it, to her jaw, her lips. Her knees threatened to give out on her, so she clung to him, her breath coming faster and faster.

I could get used to this.

Except that she couldn't. Not really.

Sawyer must've sensed her hesitation because he straightened and peered into her eyes. "You know I don't expect anything from you, right?" He ran his fingers down her arm and then took her hand. "I don't only want one thing from you..."

"I'm sorry, that was too harsh. I was just..." The hurt from yesterday rose up again, tightening her chest. "I'm not looking for some big relationship, but I'm not a fling kind of girl, either."

She waited for him to tense up or run—maybe she should've listened to Paul and kept on pretending a relationship didn't matter to her, but in that moment at least, she wanted to be real. It was one thing for him to not feel the same, another to feel like she was being used.

Sawyer rubbed his thumb across her knuckles. "We can take it as slow as you want. When I'm around you I'm happier. You're funny and sweet and when I opened up about my dad... I've never been able to talk to anyone but my mom about him, and even then, I usually hold back."

Her heart expanded, pushing against the walls of her chest.

He slipped his fingers between hers. "I may not have a lot of time here, but I want to spend it all with you." He gently kissed her lips. "What do you say?"

Wasn't that the million-dollar question? With her hand in his, she was thinking she didn't want to give this up. She could pretend it didn't bother her that he was leaving soon and she'd be left nursing a broken heart. And in a way this was good, because it meant she would never have to confess to being the nerdy girl in high school that he'd blown off—all he'd ever know her as was cool and confident.

That thought was supposed to make her feel better, but instead she started questioning everything all over again. Could she do it? She took in the way his brown hair was longer and slightly wavy on top. The perfect symmetry of his features and how the creases around his mouth gave him a slightly rugged look. The green eyes that she'd always adored, which were on her now. The guy was passionate about his screenwriting and could turn a rundown house into a work of art. Not to mention funny and caring and smart…

"Sounds perfect," she said.

At this point, what was one more act?

Brynn rushed inside her place, gathering the kissing figurines. She had more than she remembered. It all started around fourteen years old, when she was in Atlanta visiting with her maternal grandparents. Grandma took her into an antique shop and there was a little ceramic boy and girl kissing, and they were so cute, Brynn *had* to buy them. So now whenever she passed a shop filled with old treasures, she looked for more. They didn't have to be people necessarily—she had two giraffes with entwined necks, their lips smooshed together as well.

She didn't have any pictures from high school out, but she considered hiding the photo albums in case, for some odd reason, Sawyer passed the bookcase and happened to pick one up. There was no way she could hold them, though, and her angel girl who paired up with the kissing devil boy figurine was about to fall to the floor.

Tightening her grip on her collection, she walked down the hall and into her bedroom. Brynn hovered the ceramic statues over her dresser, but hesitated right before letting go. What if she and Sawyer wound up in here tonight?

I'm so not ready to go there. Not that I don't want to... She glanced at the bed and saw a flash of Sawyer and her kissing there, clothes coming off one piece at a time. Her rapid pulse pounded through her head and the temperature in the room shot up.

She turned her attention back to her figurines and then dumped them on the dresser to help keep her in check.

The doorbell rang, a high-pitched electronic chime that sounded like it was about to die, and she rushed into the living room. *The Kiss* painting Paul had teased her about was still hanging on the wall, high enough it would be much easier to take down with a chair. She darted to the kitchen, grabbed hold of the top of a chair—and the doorbell rang again.

If he can't handle a picture of kissing, I guess he doesn't get to kiss me. Desperately hoping that wouldn't happen, since she was already craving the feel of his lips on hers, Brynn let go of the chair, smoothed down her hair, and blew out a long breath.

When she opened the door, a thrill shot through her stomach. The cute guy holding a pizza box with a six-pack of grape soda was there for her. He was wearing a gray T-shirt that showed off his muscular chest and arms, and his hair was damp, so he must've showered.

Crap, I probably should've showered, too. After working

in a bait shop, that fish smell permeated everything. She'd gotten so used to it, she worried she might not realize she smelled. *How could I forget an extra spritz of perfume?*

Because I was running around like a crazy person gathering kissing statues.

He leaned in and gave her a peck on the cheek, the edge of the pizza box hitting her hip. "You gonna let me in?"

"Still deciding." She ran her gaze up and down him and then smiled. "Yeah, I think you need to come in."

And even though she'd been kissing him off and on for a few weeks, she still had the thought, *Oh my gosh, Sawyer Raines is totally in my house.*

He set the soda and box of heavenly scented pizza on her coffee table and sat down on the couch. She went into the kitchen, grabbed plates and napkins, then settled in next to him, thinking he smelled as delicious as the pizza. Something woodsy and citrusy and totally guy.

He handed her a cold can of soda. "I knew you'd be sad if I didn't bring you one, even if you do mock me for it."

"I think it's kinda cute, actually."

"'Cute.' What every guy dreams of being called by a beautiful woman."

Tingly warmth wound through her, and she was sure she was grinning like an idiot. "Well, cute and very macho, of course. Drinking grape soda makes you a total nonconformist and gives you that bad-boy edge every girl looks for."

"Oh, I'm definitely a bad boy, then." He leaned in and kissed her neck, and cute flew out the window. Heat flared through her core, and she realized her kissing figurines wouldn't be enough to keep her in check. She needed the cold slap of reality. This guy, no matter how easily he set her skin on fire, would leave soon. She needed to protect herself as much as possible, and she was starting to worry that even if things went no further than kissing, she'd still be completely broken when it ended.

She cracked the tab of her soda and the noise was enough to semi-break the spell, since Sawyer took the hint like a champ. He handed her a piece of pizza and they kept the talk light for a couple of minutes.

When Sawyer went for another piece, his foot kicked a wadded piece of paper from under her couch. He bent down to pick it up, then tilted his head as he started to un-crumple the paper—and she realized it was the picture of him, torn from her yearbook.

"Oh that's"—she ripped it out of his hand—"nothing."

"Picture of an ex?"

Nervous laughter bubbled out of her mouth. "Playbill of a horrible production. The show was bad, the date was bad." She crammed the paper deep into the folds of her couch, planning on guarding it with her life. "Awful night I'd like to forget."

Sawyer eyed her, brow furrowed, and she was sure he was going to say he'd seen it and demand to know what the hell was going on. Her heartbeats were tripping over each other, the words *I can explain* on the tip of her tongue.

But then finally he sat back, another piece of pizza in his hand. "So, did you do plays in high school?"

From one tricky question to another. Brynn supposed she could get away with the truth. If he hadn't realized they'd gone to the same high school by now, her admitting to doing plays wouldn't clue him in. "I mostly did sets in high school, actually." She was about to say she only got onstage once, but considering it was the most embarrassing moment of her life, she decided not to mention it.

"I was on the football team, believe it or not."

Oh, I remember. Your jersey made your eyes even greener. "Doesn't seem that hard to believe."

"It wasn't really my thing. My dad played, so I went out

for the team to make him happy. Then he got sick, so even though I kind of wanted to quit, I kept going. Playing for him. Even though he couldn't go to the games anymore." Sawyer shrugged. "It kept me busy, though, which was good. I probably would've gotten into trouble otherwise."

Brynn lifted her soda to her lips.

"I did go to a play once during high school. Only play I've ever seen, actually, and this poor girl's skirt came down in front of the entire audience."

Mid-swig, she choked, soda caught in her throat, the bubbles burning her nose.

"It definitely made for a memorable performance."

She coughed, reaching for a napkin.

Sawyer patted her back. "You okay?"

She swiped a hand through the air. "Fine," she wheezed. "Some just went down the wrong tube. No big"—*cough*—"deal."

Her eyes watered, her throat ached, her nose still burned, and so did her cheeks. Whether or not he remembered snubbing her in the school halls, he definitely remembered the stupid play.

"Be right back." She headed to the kitchen, grabbed a cup, filled it with water, and took a couple of long pulls. She could just make out her reflection in the tiny window over the sink. For a moment, though, she didn't see current-day Brynn. She saw the girl she used to be, full of hope, marching to the beat of her own drum. And making a complete fool of herself in front of the entire school.

Had Sawyer been up front for that show? In the back? It was one of the few times she hadn't paid attention to exactly where he was, because she'd been focused on how it'd been her time to shine.

"You okay?" Sawyer asked from behind her.

She didn't spin around, simply gripped the counter

tighter, letting it dig into her palms. Well, that fun story he'd told about his one high school play experience had worked better than her embarrassment over her kissing statues. The last thing she felt like doing now was taking Sawyer into her bedroom and letting him see her in her underwear.

Why couldn't I have been cooler in high school? She told herself it was so that she'd appreciate where she was at now, but where was she? Hiding in the kitchen from the guy who hadn't thought she was cool enough either.

But she'd decided to move past that. It was just easier said than done. Especially when he was talking about the incident like a funny story, not one that had made the last few months of high school complete hell. Everywhere she went, it was, *There's McFlasher. Hey, McFlasher. What underwear do you have on today, McFlasher?*

Sawyer's arms came around her, and she could feel his strong chest against her back. She wanted to sink back against him and let go. Say it didn't matter. But thoughts were rising up, questions she wanted to know the answers to yet didn't at the same time. *What would he do right now if I told him I was that girl? Laugh? Leave? Say it didn't matter?*

And the biggest question: *Would he even like me if he knew the real me?*

• • •

Worry rose up in Sawyer, binding itself over his lungs. Even with his arms tightly around Brynn, he felt like he was somehow losing her. He focused on her breaths, in and out. In and out. A little slower each time, until they were back to normal.

"Better?"

She nodded but didn't turn around.

"Bet you're not thinking my grape soda's so cute now,

huh?"

Her shoulders relaxed. "Very funny. I don't know how I can be so bad at swallowing. You'd think after all these years I'd have it down." She turned around in his arms and looked up at him with those big hazel eyes. "Sawyer?"

The way she said his name turned his insides to mush. Not just because of her smoky voice but because it was as though his name held more weight than it did.

"I need to tell you something, but I don't know how..." She pressed her lips together and her face paled. He tensed, sure she was going to say she'd changed her mind, that she couldn't do this. She *had* been acting weird all night.

Maybe she was dating that other guy now—he didn't know how she would, because he was purposely monopolizing her time so she couldn't.

"You know Oscar Wilde?"

He blinked, catching up to the question that was so opposite of what he expected. "Not personally, no," he said, hoping to keep the mood light.

One corner of her mouth tilted up.

"Of course. You don't think I've paid enough attention to the play to realize he wrote *The Importance of Being Earnest*? Once I read through the entire thing and saw how it all fit together, he became my new hero. I've been thinking about that as I'm trying to write." Sawyer looked down at her and realized he'd gone off on a tangent. "Sorry. You were saying?"

"Well, he's got this quote that's stuck with me ever since I heard it... 'Never love someone who treats you like you're ordinary.'"

His heart thumped hard in his chest. He wasn't sure what she was saying. Was he treating her that way? "I like it." He put his hands on the sides of her waist. "Anyone who thinks you're ordinary is an idiot. I knew that the first time I laid eyes on you."

She laughed, but it wasn't a happy laugh.

"I mean… Not just the changing in the car. Onstage. From the first time I saw you up there, I couldn't take my eyes off you."

She inhaled a deep breath and then let it out. He held his own breath, feeling as though he was awaiting her judgment. Did he pass or not? If she would let him, he'd show her just how amazing he thought she was.

"What if…?" She shook her head. "Never mind. I'm starving, and the pizza's getting cold." She started to move past him, but he caught her hand.

"Just because I'm leaving soon doesn't mean you can't talk to me. Even when I go back, I hope we can keep in touch." Whoa, where did that come from? It's not like they could make a long-distance relationship work.

Could they?

His heart rate spiked from the pressure, the way it often did when he decided to bind his life to someone else's, even for a little while. But mixed in there was a glimmer of hope, too, fighting the panic, telling him it might be worth it with Brynn.

"Sure," she said, then continued toward the living room. He'd blown off enough suggestions in his life to know that was what Brynn was doing to his.

He sat next to her on the couch. "You should at least come out sometime so we can go to a Broadway play."

Holy shit, shut up! How many times had he wondered why a girl kept pushing when he was obviously trying to pull away? And now he was doing it. *What the hell's this girl done to me? I'm turning into a chick.*

But then she looked at him, and he could see the Broadway idea struck a chord. "I've always wanted to see one. I go whenever a big show comes to Charlotte, but I always wonder if it'd be different in New York."

He grabbed her hand and kissed the top of it. "Then we'll go." His brain started firing off the reasons he couldn't follow through. How he was probably moving to California and he'd need to be focused on his screenplay.

But Brynn in New York was too tempting an opportunity to pass up. He could show her all the places he loved and watch her face light up with each new experience. Dragging it out, doing a sort of half-committed thing, would only make it worse for both of them in the end. Needing someone else, and the pressure of keeping that person happy, just wasn't for him.

Still, he couldn't help holding on to the delusion of he and Brynn a little longer.

Chapter Thirteen

When the woman with the stylish blond bob came into the bait and tackle shop wearing dress slacks, a peach button-down, and a string of pearls, Brynn simply stared for a moment. Not that no women ever came in, it was just that… Actually, it was that they came in so rarely, it seemed like they were in some secret club of women who fished but didn't talk about it. The first rule of Fish Club was don't talk about Fish Club.

And they most definitely didn't look like the woman standing in the store, glancing around with a completely bewildered expression on her face. *I wonder if she accidentally came into the wrong shop?*

Brynn smiled as she approached her. "Hi, can I help you find something?"

The woman's eyes shot to Brynn. "Oh, yes, please. I'm trying to buy my son a present." She leaned in and whispered, "I need something really good. Maybe so good that he decides he wants to stick around for a while to fish instead of going back to New York. I need to remind him of what he's missing."

The mention of New York sent a jolt through Brynn. She wanted a certain guy to stick around for a while instead of going back there, too. She studied the woman. Pale blond hair, brown eyes—no significant resemblance to Sawyer that she could see. And what were the chances his mom would come in here?

With my luck, pretty good, actually.

Brynn shook her head. Sawyer was on her mind, that was all. There were millions of people living in New York, so the odds were good that there was more than one New Yorker in town right now.

"Well, if he likes fly fishing, we've got quite an assortment of poles and flies." Of course, Sawyer seemed more like the cast-and-wait, not the have-to-be-constantly-moving fisherman. Not that this was for Sawyer.

"Are those different than regular poles? His father always went with him. I don't know anything about it."

Speaking of his father in the past tense. Another piece that fit. "I think your best bet is to get some lures that are popular right now, and maybe a few that would be better for fall. That way, he might at least feel the need to come back and try them out."

Brynn spent the next twenty minutes helping Mrs. Might-Be-Sawyer's-Mom shop. When the woman handed over the credit card to pay, Brynn stared at the name—Judith Raines. A heavy rock settled in her gut. Lying to Sawyer was bad enough; lying to his mom seemed even worse. Not that she'd lied. Had she?

"You're Donna McAdams's daughter, right?"

Oh crap. This was getting stickier by the second. "I am."

"She and I are in the same knitting group." Judith leaned in. "You know, I have a son around your age. Maybe you two could go fishing together?"

The credit card slipped from Brynn's hand. She bent

down to get it and hit her head on the counter on the way up. "Damn it! Er—sorry." Well, now that she'd sworn, Mrs. Raines had probably changed her mind about this attempted setup.

"So? What do you say? He's a great guy, I swear. How about just a coffee? He's always at the Daily Grind down the street. Maybe you could swing by and look for him? He'll have his laptop out, and here..." Mrs. Raines started digging through her purse. "I have a picture of him somewhere."

This is not *happening.* "Actually, I'm kind of dating someone right now." *Your son, who doesn't know I work here and that I know a lot about fishing, and I'd rather keep it that way.*

Two creases formed between Mrs. Raines's eyebrows. "Kind of? Well, honey, then you—"

"I love him," she blurted out. The words hung in the air between them, heavy and unexpected but completely true. The realization made her light-headed. Giddy. Terrified. She'd told dozens of lies, and maybe Sawyer was falling for someone who wasn't wholly her, but none of it changed the fact that she was in love with him. *This* so *wasn't supposed to happen.*

Mrs. Raines sighed. "Oh. Well, it was worth a shot." She grabbed her bags. "Thank you so much for your help, dear. And best of luck to you and your fellow."

"Thanks," Brynn said.

She had a feeling she was going to need it.

• • •

"Mom?" Sawyer set his keys on the coffee table and wandered through the house. All the rooms were empty, but he spotted Mom outside, watering her flowers.

When he stepped out the back door, she set the hose

down in the bed with the petunias and wiped her hands. "I wasn't sure if I'd see you today. I was about to drive to the lake house and hunt you down."

Guilt tightened his stomach. Between remodeling and directing the play, he'd barely seen her the past few days. "Sorry, Ma." He stepped down the cement stairs, avoiding that cracked spot he'd tripped on every time he had to take out the trash back in high school. He'd take care of that before he left—he'd feel awful if Mom fell and broke something when it was such a simple fix. "Painting's all done, though. Just got to let it dry before I put the finishing touches in the bedrooms. And I've got someone coming on Monday to redo the outside. The place is really starting to come together."

"That's nice," she said, but the way her voice pinched and she kept her eyes away from him said something else.

"Anyway, I came over to see what you were up to today. I have rehearsal tonight, but I thought maybe we could go to lunch or maybe even catch a matinee."

"Sure, that'd be fun." She turned off the water and then turned to face him, the no-nonsense look on her face he'd gotten so often growing up, and he automatically tensed, bracing himself. "I talked to Kayla again today," Mom said.

If he'd known she'd start talking about setting him up, he might've avoided coming over a little longer. "Kayla's not going to happen, Mom." He rolled his shoulders, the muscles stiff from all the painting.

"That's what I figured," she said with a sigh. "Come on inside. I've got something for you."

Sawyer followed her to the kitchen and she handed him a box with blue, brown, and green striped wrapping paper. "You're a few months early for a birthday gift," he joked, giving the package a gentle shake. He always liked trying to guess. And as usual, Mom had padded the box too well for any of it to shift or rattle much.

"I wanted to give you something. To say thanks for coming and taking care of the house."

"You didn't have to do that."

"I wanted to. Now go on and open it."

Sawyer ripped off the paper and opened the box's lid. Inside there were enough fishing lures to keep him busy for months of nonstop fishing. "Wow, Mom. You got all the fancy stuff. Thanks so much."

She patted his arm. "So you can stick around a bit and fish."

Ah, it all makes sense now. A gift and a trick all in one.

"I also found your senior yearbook in the study while I was dusting," she continued. "It had tons of signatures from your friends—they're always asking about you, you know. I put it on your bed in case you wanted to look through it. Thought you could call some of them up while you're in town."

"Mom—"

"And I know you didn't hit it off with Kayla, but I know other girls who might be a good fit. I'll set up a time for you to meet them and—"

"I've met a girl." An amazing, beautiful girl who made him laugh and was constantly on his mind.

Mom's face lit up.

Damn it, he shouldn't have said anything. He held up his palms. "It's only temporary. I don't want you to get any ideas. We're just spending time together while we can."

A squeal escaped her lips. So much for not getting any ideas.

It was time to tell her that he'd decided he was never getting married. His stance on that had only solidified a couple months ago, when he'd broken up with Zoey for the second time. "Mom, I know you want me to settle down, but…"

Her eyebrows were raised, and she had so much hope in her expression that he couldn't do it. If that made him a wuss, so be it.

"I'm going to be leaving soon." At this point, he was starting to sound like a broken record, both with Brynn and Mom.

"Well then we should invite this girl over to have dinner with us," Mom said, as though none of his words had gotten through to her at all. They probably hadn't.

"I'm not so sure that's a good idea."

"Of course it's a great idea. I can make that bass you caught, or if she doesn't like fish, I can think of something else."

"Mom," Sawyer said softly, wanting to break the news gently. He wasn't pulling Brynn into this situation. It wasn't fair to her. Or to Mom. Or to him.

"I haven't had a good reason to make a roast lately. She's not a vegetarian, is she? You know, if she is, Mary Sue gave me a great recipe for stuffed peppers." Mom pulled a recipe book out of her cupboard. "Here it is. All cheese and veggies and—"

"Mom." Sawyer put his hands on her shoulders. "If I bring her, you'll get too attached, and it's just… I'm sorry, but it's a bad idea."

"You're not attached to her? Not even a little bit?"

His hesitation did him in. Mom hugged him tightly, and then flipped through her recipe book, nodding at the pages. "How about tomorrow night?"

"The next few days are crazy busy, for her and for me. I don't even know if *I'll* get to see her." Outside of rehearsal anyway, where he still had to pretend their relationship was strictly business.

"But you could ask?" Mom actually brought her hands up in prayer position. Oh, she was good.

"I…suppose I could ask." As soon as the words were out of his mouth he wanted to stuff them back in and return to the moment before he'd admitted to meeting Brynn in the first place.

Mom hugged him again. Then she pulled back and stared, her eyebrows raised all the way to her hairline. "Well? Aren't you going to call her?"

"Now?"

"I want to have enough time to plan."

No way he was calling with Mom watching. He walked into his old bedroom and dialed Brynn's number. When she picked up, her familiar voice wrapped around him and sent a pang of longing through his chest. He made small talk for a few minutes, enjoying how easy it was to talk with her.

He noticed the stack of books on his bed, both his yearbook and the phone book. Mom could certainly be determined when she set her mind to something, and subtlety wasn't her strong suit. But she was reaching if she thought catching up with high school friends would keep him here. Still, he couldn't help but open the yearbook to take a look.

"You okay over there?" Brynn asked.

"Yeah, great. Sorry." He sat on the bed, scanning signatures and messages from guys he'd played ball with. Girls who'd signed hearts by their names. Some people he'd hardly talked to back then and hadn't talked to since…

"Seriously, do I need to send an emergency crew?"

"Only if you're the emergency crew and you're wearing a hot nurse outfit." He knew it was a cheesy line, but he could practically hear Brynn blushing—he definitely saw it in his mind.

She cleared her throat. "We'll discuss that later. Right now, I'm working, so if you only called to embarrass me…"

Right. He'd called for a purpose. Only he was having trouble spitting out the words. The last girl he'd brought to dinner was back in high school. That was just one of the perks of living far away. Mom had always visited during times he'd been single or hiding the fact that he wasn't. He opened his mouth to explain why he'd called, but he needed to see Brynn's reaction to know if he should keep going or not. Definitely a face-to-face conversation. "Hey, how 'bout we ride to rehearsal together?"

She was silent for a moment. "But we're undercover, remember?"

"No one will know. We'll even stagger our entrances."

She laughed, and the sound immediately made him feel lighter. "How very spy-like of us."

Sawyer closed his yearbook and tapped it against his thigh. "Come on. I can pick you up at work…"

"I'll meet you at the house," she quickly said.

Her still not budging on the work details was slowly driving him crazy. He supposed he didn't have the right to demand that kind of info, but why wouldn't she tell him? Asking to have dinner with Mom was plenty for today, though. "See you then. 'Bye, sexy nurse."

"You wish," she said with a laugh.

Sawyer sat back against his wall, grinning like the love-struck fool he was. After a moment, he returned his attention to his yearbook. As he started flipping the pages, memories of classes, football practices, and parties filled his mind. There was Clarke, the fullback who Sawyer used to go fishing with, his arms around two cheerleaders, grinning at the camera. The guy was a crack up. One day they'd swam in the lake so long, each trying to one up the other, that they were completely useless the next afternoon at practice.

I wonder what he's up to. The instant he thought it, he realized Mom's attempt to get him to remember the good times wasn't a total flop. So, point taken. He was guilty of focusing on the bad memories here, the feeling of wanting to escape the pain. He'd counted down the last few months of high school, cutting ties before he'd even left. But he'd had some great times back then, too.

He continued flipping the pages, scanning familiar faces, reliving moments from the past.

. . .

"Anything you want to tell me?" Sawyer asked when they got into his car after rehearsal. The entire drive to Charlotte, he'd been quiet. Tense, almost. If she'd known riding with him would be like that, she would've insisted on driving herself, the way she should've.

Brynn's mind spun over all the possibilities. Maybe his mom had said something. But how would she know who Brynn was?

Earlier we were talking sexy nurses, then hardly talking at all. And now he's looking at me like he expects something, and I don't know what it is. "Um…"

He reached over and pulled a handkerchief with the initials E.W. on it. Somehow it'd gotten stuck to her shirt.

Brynn laughed and took it from him, holding it to her chest as if it were a treasured object. "Yes, I've met a Mister Earnest Worthington, and we're running away together. I'm sorry, but I've always wanted to love a man named Earnest. And a man with a handkerchief. So nice to know he's blown his nose, stuck it in his pocket to get even more disgusting, and then given it to me as a crusty memento of his love."

Sawyer laughed with her. "That is pretty gross. Yay to whoever invented the Kleenex."

"And killed chivalry at the same time," she said with a dramatic sigh.

"Baby, if you want a handkerchief, I'll get you one. A clean one, even."

For a moment, Brynn couldn't breathe. He'd called her baby. Happiness bubbled up in her and she leaned over and kissed his cheek. Sawyer smiled, tiny creases showing up in the corners of his eyes, and her heart pounded out an irregular rhythm. "I take it back. You're the king of chivalry. Oh, and this idea about riding together, it's pretty awesome."

Sawyer turned and gave her lips a gentle, way-too-short kiss, and then fired up the car and pulled onto the street. When they hit the freeway, he reached over and put his hand on her thigh, causing all the blood in her body to rush to that spot. The quiet was better this half of the trip, more of a content silence than awkward, tense silence.

But then Sawyer started fidgeting, his fingers tapping against her leg. "It was such a nice day today. Not too hot and not too cold."

Brynn smiled and quoted a section of dialogue from *The Importance of Being Earnest.* "Whenever people talk to me about the weather, I always feel quite certain that they mean something else. And that makes me so nervous." They were actually Gwendolyn's lines, but she'd gone over the play so many times, Brynn practically had everyone's memorized now. Inwardly she cringed, though, knowing quoting it made her a bit odd, and was one of the very things Paul had told her to avoid.

The lights of other cars filtered in through the dark, illuminating Sawyer and leaving him dark the next. The light flashed on again to show the smile on his face. "I do mean something else."

Her heart fluttered. He'd said Jack's line back to her! He got it!

She covered his hand with hers and continued with Gwendolyn's next line. "I thought so. In fact, I'm never wrong."

"It turns out, you're not wrong," he said, glancing at

her. "I've been meaning to talk to you about something all afternoon, but I keep chickening out."

A cold lump formed in Brynn's stomach. She'd rather go back to quoting play lines, because the grave tone of his voice had her imagining the worst possible scenarios.

"It's...my mom."

Oh my gosh, she did *tell him. He's figured it out.* The lump in her stomach rose, blocking her air. "I can ex—" she started, at the same time Sawyer said, "She wants to have dinner with you."

Brynn lowered her eyebrows. "Why?" she asked, her heart still pounding like the hooves of a herd of wild horses.

"Ever since I got here, she's been trying to set me up on dates."

"Ah, your mom does that, too? I thought it was just mine. Every weekend she's trying to arrange dates for me."

"She's trying to set you up with guys from California, even though you live here?"

Oops. She'd gone from dodging questions to digging herself deeper. "Um, with guys who are where I'm from." *Not a lie. Go me.* "Apparently it's in the mom manual, right after the rule about having to embarrass your kid whenever possible."

Sawyer laughed. "Apparently." He turned onto the road that'd take them home. "My mom thinks that if I meet someone here, I'll stay instead of going back to New York."

Brynn tried not to let that comment sting, but her lungs turned to cotton and a dull throb formed at her temples.

"She even bought me a bunch of really awesome fishing supplies to try to bribe me into staying," he continued.

Good thing Brynn didn't have a grape soda, or she probably would've snorted it again.

"Anyway, the last thing I wanted to do was be set up by my mom." He grabbed her hand and laced his fingers with hers. "Especially since I'm already dating the coolest girl I've ever met."

Cool. That's me. Apparently she'd done a better job keeping up the act than she realized, because it felt like all the nerdy was seeping out of her lately.

"I know it feels like a serious step, and we don't have to go for dinner."

Under normal circumstances, she would've said sure, no problem. In fact, she would be excited he wanted her to meet his mom. But she could not, under any circumstances, go without blowing her cover, and it was way too late for that now. "With the play and everything…I just don't think it's a good idea."

Sawyer's shoulders slumped and his grip on her hand loosened. "I totally get it. I promised I'd ask, though."

Brynn glanced out the window and bit her lip. "I feel like a jerk. It's not that I don't *want* to meet her. But like you said, you're leaving, and one more entanglement…"

"Hey." He squeezed her hand. "I get it."

I don't think you do. I'm already going to lose you, and if we see your mom, I'll just lose you sooner.

Sawyer pulled up in front of his house and then hurried around the car to open her door for her. "Your place or mine?"

She liked how he made sure both options included not saying good night yet. "Well, I baked earlier today, so I've got cookies, and I know all you've got at your place is water and soda for old people."

He wrapped his arms around her and nipped at her lips. "You know you love it."

"I do." *And I love you, too.* She really needed to stop thinking those kind of thoughts before she accidentally said one out loud and scared him away for good, true identity revealed or not.

• • •

Brynn instructed Sawyer to make himself at home and then headed to the kitchen. He heard her talking to her birds, who tweeted back at her like she was some kind of cartoon princess. He smiled and headed toward the couch. But then he noticed her bookshelf. He wandered over to it, reading the titles. As he scanned them, he thought back to the conversation in the car.

How am I going to break the news to Mom that Brynn's not coming to dinner?

Earlier today, he'd been in the middle of strolling down black-and-white-memory lane, perusing the pages of photos from his graduating class, when Mom had burst into his room and shoved the recipe book in his face. She'd asked for his opinion, her hopes so high they were scraping the ceiling.

And right then, he'd given up, and just hoped he could talk Brynn into going. But she'd been so set against it.

"Okay, so— What are you looking at?" Brynn asked.

He pulled his hand away from the bookshelf. He'd been so lost in thinking about Mom, he hadn't even paid attention to the last half of the titles. "You've got a lot of classic literature in here. Not much new."

"My degree was actually in literature, minor in theater." She raised the plate of cookies. "Hungry?"

His stomach growled in answer. They settled onto the couch and he bit into a cookie. Buttery and sugary and chocolaty. "Mmm. Now there's no way I can bake for you. My stuff will suck compared to this." He liked that she baked. Not that she had to, but he could envision her in her kitchen, humming, throwing herself into it, the way she did everything.

"I went through this phase where I was set on being a baker. I came up with these amazing flavor combos. I once made cherry cheesecake cookies."

"Sounds awesome."

"It should've been delicious—*should've* being the operative word. The cream cheese and cherry filling didn't combine with the flour and sugar right, and it just turned into a puddle that was burned and raw. So then I decided I was going to be a famous painter instead. Only I wasn't good at that beyond the basic, stage prop stuff. Nothing people would want to hang up in their house."

Sawyer watched her face, the way her eyes lit up and her eyebrows rose and fell, her excitement so close to the surface. All her emotions, really. Even if she didn't tell him what was going on, he could read her. Which was how he realized she was getting attached, despite her saying she was fine with their current arrangement. Guilt pinched his gut, eating away at the lightness he felt just from being around her.

"I was obsessed with creating," she continued, a smile curving her beautiful lips. "But I'd always change my mind on exactly what I wanted to create. I even tried writing a tragic sweeping romance."

He brushed her bangs aside and pushed his fingers into her silky hair. "And how'd that go?"

"Well, there were ball gowns and social classes and betrayal—of course. A banished aristocrat girl and a guy who was willing to do anything to be with her..." She glanced at him, then shook her head and took a bite of cookie.

"Don't stop," he said, sliding his hand behind her neck. "You could talk forever for all I care."

She smiled. "That's what you say now. You have no idea how long I can go on about tragic love stories. Like I said, I do have a degree in literature." She took another bite and he got distracted watching her mouth. She yawned. "Man, I'm exhausted."

Maybe that was a hint for him to leave, but he wasn't going to until she straight up said it or kicked him out. He was selfish and he knew it, but he only had a little bit of time left with this amazing woman. And despite his attempts to remain un-invested in them as a couple, he realized he was getting pretty attached himself. He put his arm around her and leaned back on the couch. Brynn rested her head on his shoulder, and he pulled her closer, taking her weight onto him. He could feel her curves under the thin material of her shirt. He wanted to make a move so badly, but last night when kissing had been turning into more, she'd pulled away.

Sawyer ran his fingers down her back, enjoying the way she pushed into him—she was ticklish. He wanted to test out every inch. He swallowed hard, working for control. "So, what was after writing?"

"Acting." She smiled. "That one stuck, though I still try baking experiments or pottery or whatever hits me now and then. A few months ago, I was determined to learn French. But I didn't get very far." She tilted her head up. "Enough about me," she said, and her lips brushed his jaw, making him fight back a groan. "Is writing screenplays it for you?"

He readjusted, settling into the corner of the couch and tugging Brynn closer. Her hair smelled like some kind of flower, and her hand was high enough on his thigh he was having trouble focusing. "I've thought of different careers over the years, especially after I got rejection after rejection. But when my screenplay was made into a movie, it was amazing. Granted, there were a few parts I was a little disappointed in, because they weren't what I'd envisioned. I guess that's all part of the biz, though."

"You should direct them, then. You'd be a great director."

Sawyer thought of the play now, how it was all coming together, so much better than the first day he walked into the tiny theater. He liked picking apart what wasn't working and making it better. Liked the control, too, honestly. "I don't know. Maybe."

"You know, they film some movies in North Carolina… TV shows, too. More in Wilmington than here, though. There was that *One Tree Hill* show. And *Dawson's Creek*. I'm sure there are more…adult things."

"Adult things?"

She smacked his chest—or attempted to, anyway. Her breaths were slowing, and her eyelids were drifting closed. "I'm saying there are other options. If you want them."

It *was* the digital age. He could write from anywhere, really, despite what his agent claimed about opportunity in California. The one thing he had on his side was that he'd already sold a script and the one he was writing now did have interest—if he could just finish it and get it to his agent. He'd also done script doctoring for screenplays that weren't quite working, which, again, he could do anywhere. If he chose to live somewhere else—like North Carolina—he'd have to travel from time to time. But if it meant having Brynn to come home to…

He couldn't think like that. Because he still wasn't getting married or having kids. While he liked how animatedly she talked about her attempt at writing a romance, it was just another reminder that she wanted a relationship like that in real life. Maybe not the ball gowns or betrayal, but she wanted more than he could give her.

"Brynn?" he said.

No response. He shifted enough so that he could see her face. His heart expanded and filled up entirely with her. He recognized the emotion stirring from somewhere deep inside, only he'd never felt it on this level before. He tried to tell himself it was too soon, but it didn't matter, because there was no denying it now.

"I love you," he whispered. "And I'm sorry I can't be the man you need me to be."

Chapter Fourteen

Brynn darted into the shop two minutes before it was time to open. Paul crossed his arms and shot her a look.

"I know, I know," she said. "I'm sorry." The fishing channel was already playing, the rotund guy onscreen sitting in his boat, getting ready to explain how he trolled for trophy-sized fish. She didn't even care that she'd seen this very episode enough times she could quote it. Because this morning she'd woken up in Sawyer's arms. As they'd been lying on the couch, she'd even stolen a couple of seconds to study the faint scar that crossed his eyebrow, his full bottom lip, and the dip just above his upper one.

When they'd said their good-byes on her front porch, he'd drawn her close, kissed her neck, and said, "I liked sleeping with you."

Even though she knew he was teasing her, it'd sent heat traveling up her core. The entire drive here, it'd been all she could think about—the possibility of what it'd be like if she actually took that step with him.

"It's starting to be an everyday thing," Paul said, pulling

her out of Happy Vibes Land. "I've done all the pre-open stuff by myself for the last three days."

She wanted to suggest they have one of the other workers come in to help, but she knew they had to be careful with hours. "Once the play's done, I'll go back to normal, I swear." Only then she'd probably be spending her nights crying into a carton of ice cream, watching sappy movies because she missed Sawyer. But after she cried herself to sleep, she'd wake up early and make up for the past few weeks of slacking off.

"Normal." Paul huffed, but she let it go so they wouldn't have a fight. She also decided not to mention that she'd promised Dani she'd meet her and her in-laws at the bridal shop this afternoon and needed to take a *slightly* longer lunch break.

The day dragged a bit, though the shop was busy. Finally, when they hit a lull, Brynn leaned on the counter next to Paul. "So, how are things with Carly?" She figured that'd put a smile on his face. He'd been going on and on about her even more the past few days.

"I swore that I wouldn't let my guard down again, but… Carly makes me feel important. Needed." Paul twisted to face Brynn. "I know I told you to hold back and not to let the guy know how much you like him, but…I think I was wrong. If you like that guy, you should tell him. If it's right, you won't scare him off."

Brynn scuffed the floor with her shoe. "What about the fact that he thinks I'm someone else?"

"Oh, I'm sure you haven't done that good a job of hiding the fact that you're a weirdo." He grinned at her.

"Gee, thanks."

"You should probably tell him the truth. See what happens."

"Yeah, maybe." Panic rose up, binding her lungs, as she thought about coming completely clean. Maybe he'd understand, but what would she do if he didn't? "I think I better wait until after the play's done. Like right before he leaves. That way, I won't screw up what has the potential to be the best week of my life."

"Not to get all mushy, but you know that I'd be lost trying to keep this place going without you. You're smart and you're funny. Don't settle for less than you deserve."

Tears gathered in her eyes.

Paul shook his head at her. "Ah, hell. I knew I should've kept my mouth shut."

She hugged him despite the fact that he looked like he wanted to run. Who knew if he'd ever say anything so nice to her again? "I hope you and Carly work out." She was surprised that she actually meant it.

A couple of customers wandered in—one old man frowned at Brynn and Paul like hugging was against the law—and she got back to work. But her thoughts kept returning to Sawyer. Every minute with him held this sense of urgency, the days they had left slipping through her fingers. He made her feel like no one else ever had. She loved him, and she didn't want to be filled with regrets when he left. She wanted to experience everything with him. At least no matter what happened after that, she'd be able to hold on to one perfect night together.

While courage was pumping through her veins, she got out her phone and sent a text to Sawyer.

You. Me. A nice dinner out, and dessert at my place after. What do you say?

Within a minute, he'd texted back.

YES

Excitement zipped through her stomach. Tonight, she

was going to go all out with her I'm-a-confident-girl-who-gets-what-I-want persona, and seduce her sexy sorta-boyfriend.

• • •

Sawyer loaded the last of the furniture into the truck he'd borrowed from Mom's neighbor so he could finish clearing the big items out of the house. The attic, and even a few of the bedrooms, had antique pieces that'd been left there all these years. He kept a rocking chair for reasons he couldn't explain—he wasn't going to take it to New York, and he wasn't exactly a rocking-chair type of guy. Still, it was beautiful and handcrafted, and he couldn't bring himself to add it to the rest of the furniture he planned on selling off.

He got into the truck and headed toward Quality Antiques. As he drove, he thought of Brynn, like he'd been doing since first thing that morning. He couldn't wait to go out with her tonight. He wasn't sure if she'd meant what it sounded like when she'd said "dessert at my place," but he knew how he wanted the night to end. And not just because sex with her would be great, but because... Well, damn it, because he loved her. No denying it anymore. The girl shone like the sun, high energy and bright, her enthusiasm for life impossible not to catch. She named birds after literary characters. She was the most unique, beautiful woman he'd ever known. He wanted to wrap her in his arms and never let her go; he wanted to run his fingers across all her curves without any annoying fabric in the way.

He reached over and cranked up the air conditioning. Tonight was too far away. He parked the truck in the side alley by the shop, the way they'd told him to when he'd called about selling the items earlier. The owner came out, they haggled over price for a few minutes, and then he helped the woman load it into her shop.

As he was walking toward the front of the store, he noticed a tiny, circular, cream-colored music box with a black and white outline of two people dancing. There were musical notes in a line around it and a large red heart. Sawyer picked it up and spun the tiny crank on the side. The top was covered in a small metal grate, and inside, he could see the tiny parts spinning as music filled the air.

It made him think of Brynn, and he decided she needed to have it. He took it to the register and asked Mrs. Marts to take it out of the money for the furniture. As she counted the bills, Sawyer was counting the time he had left here. If he stuck to the plan, he'd be leaving in less than a week.

He'd definitely lost focus on his screenplay lately—he really should get back to his normal life. But with the play taking up the weekend, that didn't leave much time to wrap up the last details on the house and get it listed. He also wanted to fit in as much time with his mom and Brynn as possible. Although he wasn't sure how he was going to balance that.

He let out a long breath. Another week wouldn't kill him. Maybe two. He could be stricter about his writing, and he wouldn't be spending every night at rehearsals. Plus, if he stayed longer, he could see where he and Brynn stood at the end of the month. A little more time, and maybe...Well, maybe he could promise her more than here and now.

He couldn't believe he was thinking it. Not after Zoey. *Oops*, he realized, *I never called her back*. He didn't want to deal with her now, though. Before their relationship, he'd been hesitant of commitment, but ever since he thought he would have to be with her forever, he'd known true fear of settling down. Especially after that day she'd dragged him into the bridal shop.

"Just come on," Zoey had said, tugging him inside.

"I thought I couldn't see the dress before..." He hadn't been able to say "the wedding." A month ago she'd been throwing dishes at his head as he broke up with her. Then she was leaving, alternating "I hate you" and "I still love you" messages.

And now… He'd gulped, his stomach rolling. He hadn't even asked her. He supposed he'd have to now. It was the right thing to do. His lungs collapsed and his skin itched like it was breaking out in hives.

"I don't believe in all that," Zoey had said. "And besides, I've had my eye on this dress for months."

Months? "You've been coming in here for that long?"

"Newsflash, women like weddings. We think about the dress and the day and how the guy will finally ask us." She'd given him a pointed look that said, *You'd better be asking me soon, buddy.*

Zoey let out a squeal. "It's still here." She lifted a white dress—he didn't notice details, just white and fluffy with a side of Lifetime of Regret.

"Maybe we should wait until after—"

"No way. Who knows how long it'll take me to get my body back. I want to wear this one while I can."

All the air had been sucked out of the room. Sawyer thought of his dad. What would Dad have told him? Sawyer could hear the lecture on responsibilities and doing the right thing. And as soon as he told his mom, she'd be so happy she probably wouldn't even notice he wasn't.

Sawyer scratched at his skin. "Just…get whatever you want. I've got to grab a drink."

"Mr. Raines?" called out a voice.

Sawyer shook off that bad memory and focused on the bag in Mrs. Marts's hand. "Thanks."

Like that day with Zoey, he felt like he could use a drink. He decided to grab some lunch from the deli a few shops over before he headed back. For such a tiny thing, the bag with Brynn's present suddenly felt heavy. He lifted it, wondering if he was getting in too deep. Minutes ago he'd been thinking about trying to make it work long-term, but one memory of Zoey and he was questioning his desire to get into a relationship again.

He needed to get over it, though. Brynn wasn't like that. She wasn't someone who'd lie to his face, the way his ex had.

· · ·

Brynn sat in the bridal shop with Wes's mom, Kathleen, and his sisters, Audrey and Jill, as they waited on Dani to come out of the dressing room. When Dani had met Brynn out front, she'd said, "I need your help. I love Wes's family, but they seriously don't get when I say I want simple. So your job is to help me find a dress that doesn't have any bows and isn't foofy, or glittery, or lacey."

"So basically you want a tux," Brynn had teased.

Dani's eyes widened, the cool collected girl she was normally, nowhere in sight.

Brynn had put her hand on Dani's arm and said, "No worries. We'll find you something perfect." They'd scoured the store and come up with three options, which Dani was trying on now.

The door to the dressing room swung open. When Dani stepped out, a collective gasp went through the room. It did have lace, but it was a sheer overlay and had cute lace cap sleeves. Dani spun, showing off the keyhole back.

"Wes did ask me to look for a backwards dress," she said, peering over her shoulder into the mirror. She smiled. "I think this counts."

"It's, seriously, perfect for you," Brynn said.

"Amazing," Audrey added.

Jill nodded, a huge smile on her face. "I think that's it."

Kathleen started to cry.

Within twenty minutes, they were all leaving the store, Dani's dress ordered—she said why try on any others when she'd found the one. Brynn and Dani waved good-bye to Wes's family.

"Thanks so much for coming to help out," Dani said. "I never thought I'd get this excited about a dress, but— Ah! I'm so freakin' stoked!"

Brynn laughed. She glanced down the sidewalk—she really needed to get back to the shop. But she froze when she saw Sawyer step out of the antique store. He glanced up, and when his eyes met hers, her entire body broke out in pleasant chills.

He walked up and gave her a hug. His gaze moved to the doorway they'd barely come out of and his face fell. "Do you, uh, work, there?" He swallowed and it seemed like it took a lot of effort.

"No, we were wedding dress shopping," Brynn said.

He scratched at his arm, his eyes darting around like a caged animal.

"I mean, Dani was shopping. I was just helping. Remember Dani?"

Sawyer glanced at her. "Oh, right. Hi."

"I'm getting married in a couple of months," Dani said, and Sawyer seemed to go a shade whiter. It would've been funny if it didn't make Brynn's stomach take a nosedive. Maybe a small part of her had thought that Sawyer would stay in North Carolina. Not that she was ready for wedding bells, but he was staring at the bridal shop as if it'd been responsible for everything wrong with the world.

"I'll catch you later," Dani said. "Thanks again. And next week we'll go shopping for your br—" She looked at Sawyer, tilted her head, and then smiled at Brynn. "Beer."

So Brynn wasn't the only one noticing he was freaking out. She was glad Dani diverted the conversation, though.

"Yes, beer shopping. Can't wait."

Brynn hooked her arm through Sawyer's and tugged him away from the bridal shop. "So dress rehearsal tonight, and then you and I are going out for a nice dinner. You still good with that?" She held her breath, nerves dancing around her stomach.

Sawyer nodded. "Yeah. Sure."

Brynn could feel herself losing him. She'd work extra hard tonight. No acting like she cared about relationships. No confessing that she cared about him or needed him— especially no admitting she loved him. "I've got to get back to work."

She waited for him to ask about it like he usually did— she'd decided she would say she worked at a tourist shop and her boss was coming down on her lately, which was mostly true.

But Sawyer only nodded and said, "See you later."

She leaned in for a quick kiss. When she pulled back, Sawyer caught her arm. His features relaxed, and he seemed to morph back to normal. "I'm sorry, I was…somewhere else for a minute." He leaned down and gave her a proper kiss, with lips and the perfect amount of tongue. She drank him in, from the feel of her body fitted to his, to the way his fingers tangled in her hair.

"That was much better," she said against his lips, eyes still closed. She felt him smile, and electric zips fired through her body. Never in her life had anything felt so right. And she knew she had to hold onto that while she could. It was all that mattered. She'd show him—show herself—that she could be the kind of girl to turn a guy's head and make him drool a little.

Tonight, she was embracing the siren persona hiding in the deepest corners of herself. She'd worry about what happened after…well…after.

Chapter Fifteen

After a thirty-minute fight with a flat iron, Brynn's hair was shiny and sleek. The red dress she'd put on was low-cut, several inches above her knee, and nowhere close to anything someone in the Victorian Era would wear. If she had, she would've been shunned by high society. And low society. Basically, major shunning all around.

The transformation was so extreme that Brynn barely recognized herself. That happened from time to time during dress rehearsals or when she saw pictures from the theater productions she'd put on. But this person was half her. The half of her that was getting lucky tonight.

She glanced at her immaculate bedroom. She'd almost lost her mind and put flowers and candles around her bed, but that didn't say she was the kind of girl who could sleep with a guy and then shrug it off if he didn't call.

Oh my gosh, what if he doesn't call me after?

Her hands shook, and this time when she looked in the mirror, she saw the girl Sawyer had turned down when she asked him to prom. The girl who made a fool of herself in front of guys. The girl who snort-laughed occasionally and spilled food on her clothes and— Her lungs strained for air and the room spun.

No, no, no. I'm not that *Brynn tonight.* She closed her eyes, the way she always did before the curtain rose for the first time. When the audience was about to be introduced to someone who wasn't her.

Think Lola from Damn Yankees.

Whatever Lola wants, Lola gets…

Another deep breath, the curtain was rising and… Brynn opened her eyes and smiled at Lola in the mirror. Just in time, because the shrill doorbell rang.

Time to go make Sawyer drool.

• • •

Sawyer ran a hand down his navy button-down shirt, hoping he wasn't overdressed. Brynn had said a nice dinner. He noticed her porch light was sagging, a breath away from falling off the wall completely. He'd come over and fix that tomorrow while she was at—

Brynn opened the door and he forgot what he was thinking. Hell, he forgot his name. And how to speak, apparently.

The fiery red dress hugged her body in all the right places and showed off her legs. Her lips curved into a seductive smile as she leaned one hip on the doorframe, looking like some kind of sexy she-devil. His heart hammered against his ribs and he was tempted to just push her back through the door and carry her to her bed.

Gone was the girl you took home to meet your mom. This was the kind of girl you tried to hit on—the one who brushed you off with a sneer. He liked it, but it seemed so… not like Brynn, and he wasn't sure how to take that. But then he was lost in cleavage and all that creamy skin.

She stepped so close he could feel her breath on his neck. "Are you ready?"

He stifled a groan. Yeah. He was ready. Not for dinner so much, though.

Her large eyes lifted to his and there was a flash of the Brynn he was used to there, a hint of vulnerability swimming in the green and brown.

"You look amazing," he said. "Absolutely stunning."

The seductress was back in an instant. She placed both hands on his chest and brushed her lips across his. "Let's go, then."

When she started down the steps he let out a shaky breath. Holy shit. He wasn't going to be able to drive, much less walk into a restaurant if he didn't get himself under control. Which meant he should probably stop staring at her ass.

Sawyer rushed down the sidewalk, opened the car door for her, and bit the inside of his cheek when he stared down at her bare legs. As he drove toward the restaurant, he thought a hundred times about putting his hand on her thigh, but knew it'd ruin the control he was barely hanging on to. Apparently the woman wanted him completely unraveled tonight, and it was definitely working.

As they walked into Dressler's Restaurant, he put his hand on the small of her back, wanting everyone to know she was with him. Still not quite believing it himself. Within a few minutes, they were seated.

Sawyer glanced around the upscale restaurant. "I've only been here once before. Right before prom my junior year."

Brynn's smile faltered.

He put his hand over hers. "Already this night's much better."

She just blinked at him a few times, and he noticed she looked a little paler than usual.

"Brynn, are you okay?"

"I'm great." She straightened in her chair and swiped her hair behind her ear. He still couldn't get over how different she looked. It almost felt like he was cheating on her with… her. And again, he wasn't complaining, but she'd hardly said a thing the entire drive, which wasn't like her. His nerves were starting to bounce around inside his gut, but his hormones were still firing at full speed, and the combination was giving him heart palpitations.

The waiter came and took their order, and when Sawyer turned back, Brynn leaned her elbow on the table and licked her lips. He almost tipped over his glass of water reaching for it. He finally got it to his lips—right as she slid the toe of her shoe up the inside of his leg.

He choked down a gulp and wiped his mouth with the back of his hand. "Um, I…" He reached into his pocket and withdrew the miniature music box. "I saw this today and thought of you." He set it on the table in front of her.

Brynn picked it up. Her eyes lit as she turned the box from side to side, studying the images. Then she cranked the handle and the tinny music came out, slow and steady. His Brynn appeared in that moment, the smile that brought out her cheeks and the uninhibited excitement over something so small. His heart swelled. There was the girl he fell in love with.

He swallowed. He wanted to tell her.

But he didn't want to tell her.

She deserved to know.

"I…"

Brynn pushed away from the table so quickly, she teetered on her black high heels. "I'll be right back."

Are those tears in her eyes?

"Brynn," he said, starting to stand.

She waved him off. "I'm fine. I've just gotta go find the

restroom."

He slowly settled into his seat again. The music box sat between the gleaming silverware on her side of the table. Now he was even more confused. She liked it, right? Was this one of those times when tears were a good thing?

• • •

Brynn used a tissue to dab her eyes, trying to wipe the tears without making a mess of her mascara. "What are you doing?" she asked the girl in the mirror. "Lola doesn't cry."

Out of the corner of her eye, she caught the wide-eyed expression of a woman reflected over her shoulder. The lady washed her hands in the other sink, glancing at Brynn like she might attack at any moment, and then rushed out of the bathroom, her heels clicking against the tile.

"No, what am *I* doing?" Brynn dropped her head back. At first it was fun seeing Sawyer's awestruck expressions, thrilling to know she could actually have that kind of effect on a man. But it was so much damn work, and she didn't feel connected with reality anymore. Not in the way she used to in high school, though, where her own world was a nice place— the kind of romance found in novels, and chivalry wasn't dead. This was the kind where *she* felt like fiction.

She boosted herself onto the sink and took a few deep breaths. As much as she wanted to seduce Sawyer—not just to prove she could, but also because she wanted to take that next step with him—this wasn't who she was.

Another woman came inside, gave Brynn an uneasy glance, and bolted into a stall. *Nope, I don't belong here. I'm not this girl.*

The sensation of cold wetness against her skin made Brynn shoot off the counter, so fast her stupid high heels slipped on the tile. She had to brace herself on the wall to keep from going down, but she was too late—she could feel the wet fabric on the seat of her dress.

Maybe it won't be noticeable.

Brynn stood on tiptoe to study her backside in the mirror. Yep, there she was: the girl who sat in water and had a large wet spot on her butt.

Thanks for the reminder of who I truly am, universe.

She punched on the hand dryer and scooted under it.

On the bright side, the music box Sawyer gave her proved that he knew the real her. The one who loved antique treasures and kissing. Those blessed butterflies rose up, floating and spreading warmth through her entire body. She loved Sawyer Raines.

And he certainly acted like he loved her back.

All the doubts that'd been holding her back disappeared, and a weight lifted from her shoulders.

The woman came out of the stall, and instead of avoiding eye contact or hanging her head in shame, Brynn flashed her a wide smile and waved. She laughed when the woman took off without even washing her hands—not very sanitary. The dryer went off and she punched it again.

The more Brynn thought about it, the more sure she became. She'd fooled herself about love before, had told herself lies so she could try to make it work with decent guys. But what she and Sawyer had was real. Her heart spoke to his, and his to hers. He was the guy she'd been waiting for.

A dozen happy emotions swirled through her. She did one more check—the fabric looked dry, even though it felt a bit damp.

Time to drop the act.

She was going to get the guy, and she was going to get him by being herself.

• • •

Sawyer wiggled his foot, tapping it against the leg of the table in a steady rhythm. He worried Brynn was crying in the bathroom and he was just sitting out here like a chump. Of course, he didn't want to be the chump who went into the ladies' bathroom, either. He was giving her one more minute. Then he'd at least find a female employee to go check on her.

He glanced at the time and started to scoot out his chair. Then he spotted her winding her way around tables, coming toward him. She looked like the same girl he'd picked up, yet somehow she was back to herself. Smiling shyly when he caught her eye. Man, he loved her. He wasn't sure what to do about it, but when he was with her, the world made more sense.

He stood, planning on going old school and pulling out her chair in for her. But then someone stepped into her path. An older gentleman with white hair, who started talking to her.

"Raines?" someone asked from behind him.

Sawyer turned toward the voice.

"It is you! How the hell you doing, man?" Dirk Markham, the quarterback of the high school football team, clapped him on the back. A couple of the cheerleaders used to refer to him as Dirk the Jerk, and Sawyer remembered thinking the title fit pretty well. "I heard you were some big-shot movie guy now."

"I dabble, anyway."

"So how long are you in town? We should at least grab a beer."

Sawyer didn't want to be having this conversation. With most anyone else from the team, sure, but not a guy he could barely stand in high school. He wanted to get back to Brynn. He could see she was trying to break away from the elderly gentleman talking to her.

"Holy shit." Dirk ran his eyes up and down Brynn, and Sawyer's blood heated. He cleared his throat.

Dirk looked at him and then back to Brynn. "Dude, are you here with McFlasher? Not that I'd blame you. I mean, who knew she'd turn out hot? She's still got those big fish eyes, but if she'd like to drop her skirt again, I could definitely help her with that." He nudged Sawyer in the ribs with his elbow.

Brynn moved around the man she'd been talking to. Her face paled when her gaze landed on Dirk. She took a few fast steps toward the table. "Sawyer."

McFlasher. Sawyer's brain was trying to put the puzzle pieces together. Where had he heard that bef— It hit him hard, a bolt to the mind. High school. The girl in the play. Everyone started calling her McFlasher after that.

No. Way.

"You're from...here?" he asked Brynn, his eyes locked onto hers.

"Looks like we've got our own little high school reunion going on," Dirk said.

Sawyer could see Brynn retreating into herself, the way she had when he'd first met her. She wrapped her arms around her shoulders and lowered her head. "I can explain." She glanced at Dirk. "Once we're alone."

Dirk held up his hands. "I can take a hint." He nudged Sawyer with his elbow again. "Good luck, man." He started to retreat and then spun around. "See you around, McFlasher."

Brynn closed her eyes, her skin a deathly sheet of white now.

Sawyer placed his palms on the table and leaned in. "What the hell is going on? You went to high school with me?"

Brynn's eyes met his, a challenge inside of them. "What?" she asked, her voice quivering. "You don't remember?"

"No. I mean, I remember seeing that play. Hell, I told you about it."

Her eyes shone, tears gathering in the corners. "The play. That's all you remember, don't you?"

He threw his hands up. "Am I supposed to remember more? I didn't even know that *was* you until two seconds ago."

She closed her eyes and a tear ran down her cheek. Instinctively, he wanted to reach up and brush it away. A few minutes ago, he would've. But right now his mind was too busy spinning with the fact that they went to high school together.

Which meant…she wasn't from LA.

Anger wound its way up his body, sending hot bursts of blood through his veins. "What game are you playing here? Why didn't you tell me before that you knew me?"

"*Why?*" She gave a mirthless laugh. "You wanna know why?" She gestured in the direction Dirk had gone. "You think I want to be called McFlasher for the rest of my life? To live my worst moment over and over?"

Another tear slipped down her cheek. "Or how about the time I asked you to prom back in high school? It took me days to work up the courage to talk to you. And when I asked, you just shook your head and walked away like I wasn't even worth five minutes of your time. Gee, why would I *not* want to relive that?"

A clashing mix of sympathy, bitterness, and confusion was rising through him. "I don't remember any of that."

Brynn clenched her jaw. "Of course you don't."

"Don't turn this on me. *You're* the one who lied. You said you were from LA."

She sniffed. "No, you assumed I was from there; I just let you. I didn't think I'd keep talking to you. Or start dating you." She lifted her eyes to his again. "Or…fall in love with you."

His heart dropped. All the air shot from his lungs.

The waiter chose that moment to come with the food. He set it on the table. "Sir? Ma'am? Don't you want to sit down?"

Brynn settled into her chair; Sawyer remained standing.

"Anything else I can get for you?" the waiter asked.

"No thanks," Sawyer said, harsher than he'd meant to. He turned back to Brynn. "How can you even...? I can't..." His heart was somewhere near his stomach now, but it felt like it was being ripped in two. How dare she tell him she loved him. Especially after that information bomb she'd dropped. No, *she* hadn't even dropped it. Dirk had.

Sawyer could feel the walls closing in, the suffocating tentacles wrapping around his lungs. "I'm going back to New York. I always told you I was."

Pain flickered through her eyes. Or maybe she was just that good of an actress. "That's what you have to say to me?"

"I don't know *what* to say. I thought I knew you, but I don't." He shook his head. "I think maybe this whole thing was a mistake."

"Sawyer. Don't." Brynn stood so fast her chair rocked back but didn't quite tip. People were starting to stare and whisper now. She glanced around and then moved next to him. He watched her chest rise and fall. Rise and fall. "Maybe I didn't tell you the whole truth, but don't tell me you don't know me. You're one of the few people in this world who does." She reached out a hand and placed it over his heart. "You have to feel something between us. I can't be the only one who feels like this."

She locked eyes with him. "Tell me I'm not."

He heaved a sigh. Her hurt expression from earlier flashed before his eyes. He could see how much Dirk's words had cut her, and yes, he could see why she wouldn't want to admit something like that. But his walls were back up, and he wasn't sure he could let them down again.

Out of the corner of his eye, Sawyer noticed the older gentleman Brynn had been talking to approach the table. "Are you okay, dear?"

Brynn glanced at him and wiped the tears from her cheeks. "I'm fine. Thanks, Howard."

The man narrowed his eyes at Sawyer, then turned back to Brynn. "I'll check on you when I come into the shop tomorrow." He either said it loud to let Sawyer know, or he was nearly deaf. This whole scene was turning into a spectacle, and Sawyer was waiting for someone to come kick them out. The man patted Brynn's shoulder. "Save me your best batch of night crawlers. I'm planning on catching some big fish tomorrow."

"Night crawlers?" Sawyer said when they were alone again.

Brynn bit her lip. "Right. So…I work at Bigfish Bait and Tackle shop. I sort of… Well, my family owns it. My brother and I run it now."

"You run a bait and tackle shop? So when we went fishing…?" Irritation rose up in him again. "Damn, Brynn, is anything you told me real?"

"It's not a big deal. Just a few minor details that—"

"Not a big deal?" he asked, stepping back. "You lied to me about everything. What are you trying to do? Get me to stay? You thought I'd move here and then you'd spring the truth on me?"

"Of course not. I was planning on telling you, I just didn't know how."

She was *exactly* like Zoey. Manipulative and a liar. "I don't want to hear it." He took some bills from his wallet and tossed them on the table. "I'm done."

Chapter Sixteen

This wasn't how tonight was supposed to go. The beautiful dishes with their artfully presented food blurred as tears filled Brynn's eyes. She'd told him she loved him.

And he walked away.

A hole opened up in her chest, and warm tears slipped down her cheeks. *He was out of my league anyway.* She'd spent years telling herself that the people she'd gone to high school with didn't matter. In a lot of ways, she still felt like that. But Sawyer mattered.

Every breath was like inhaling glass, every sound too loud. She couldn't move, but she didn't want to stay here, surrounded by elegant people, tears running down her face. She didn't want to think about how awkward the play would be tomorrow—opening night. And the two shows on both Saturday and Sunday. No matter how good an actress she was, she wouldn't be good enough to not see Sawyer and feel the stab of rejection. He'd discarded her heart, the same way he'd done in high school.

Fool me once, shame on you. Fool me twice, and I guess I

deserve to have my heart ripped out of my chest, stomped on, and put back in all mangled.

Brynn forced herself to place one foot in front of the other and head toward the exit. She could call a taxi, but she didn't want to go home, where she'd have to see Sawyer's house and possibly him. No doubt she'd start thinking about him and end up doing something desperate and/or stupid.

She pulled out her cell and hit speed dial number one.

"Hey," she said when he answered. "I need you to come get me."

• • •

Sawyer kicked the trashcan on the sidewalk, then swore when pain shot up his toe, into his shin. As soon as he'd left the restaurant, he just started walking, hoping… He didn't know, that he'd stop feeling so pissed. That he'd get Brynn's hurt expression out of his head.

That he'd blink and this would all be a nightmare and he'd still be sitting across from her, talking about how she wrote tragic romances between baking experiments and painting. Or quoting play lines back and forth.

Thinking about how much he loved her.

I don't love her. I love a figment. A character.

A very beautiful character with pretty eyes and perfect skin and a smile that makes everything seem like it'll be okay. He kept seeing her face. Laughing. Smiling. Looking at him like he was somebody she needed in her life.

She'd made him want to stay here.

He clenched his fists, his insides turning cold and hard. He'd opened up to her about his dad, and she hadn't even bothered telling him the truth. He eyed the trashcan, wanting to kick it again. He needed to destroy something.

Brynn, the girl he'd thought was so different from his ex,

ended up trying to trap him, just like Zoey had. He couldn't let that go. He'd learned the hard way that one lie led to another.

He remembered the relief he'd felt after breaking up with Zoey the first time. With every crazy message she sent, whether it was the hate-filled rants or the begging to take her back, he'd think, *Thank God I got out of that before it was too late.*

But then she'd sent a very different message.

He could still remember the way his heart had stopped when he read the text.

I'm pregnant.

Zoey had told him she was on the pill—he'd asked several times, always willing to use extra protection if needed. The last thing he was ready for was a baby. He'd never wanted to have kids because it meant they'd need the most stable home life possible, and that meant actually committing his life to someone. Zoey wasn't who he'd had in mind for a wife even if he *was* going to go that route, but what was he supposed to do? If she was going to have his baby, he couldn't just leave her.

So he'd reconciled with her, fighting back bitterness that he was stuck in the situation every single time he'd look at her. He tried to make himself love her—focus on all her good qualities—but he'd felt himself shutting down, living life on miserable autopilot.

At the premiere of his movie, Zoey was on his arm, looking stunning in a silver dress. To the casual observer, they were the picture-perfect couple, and he plastered on a smile, playing the part. That night, Sawyer started remembering the reasons he'd liked Zoey in the first place. She talked him up, made him feel good about his movie, and she was driven and smart. He decided he needed to accept his life and find a way to enjoy it. For the first time, her pregnancy didn't seem like a burden instead of a reason to celebrate. He started picturing a son or daughter to carry around. And, eventually, watch movies with, the way he'd done with his dad.

Then the after party came, and he noticed Zoey was downing champagne. Some of the actors and crewmembers from her new television series were there, too, and they were surrounding her, drinking and laughing. When Sawyer tried to subtly tell her to cool it with the alcohol, she laughed and grabbed another drink. When he blurted out that it wasn't good for the baby, her coworkers' mouths had dropped.

Her producer and agent were there, and when they'd erupted in questions about how this was going to work with her TV shooting schedule, she finally confessed that she wasn't pregnant. Had never *been* pregnant.

Sawyer saw red that night. It was all he could do not to tell her right then and there in front of everyone what a manipulative bitch she was.

While she packed her belongings, she cried and begged him to give her another shot, but there was no way he could be with someone who'd tried to trick him into being with her.

• • •

Paul eyed Brynn as she got into the car. "I said to be yourself, not dress like a hooker."

Brynn blinked at the tears, but they started pouring all over again. She was sure her mascara had relocated to her cheeks.

"Shit, I'm sorry. That was supposed to be a joke." He patted her on the shoulder. "Whose ass do I need to kick?"

Brynn leaned her head back. "It was my fault. All the lies finally caught up to me. And now that Sawyer knows who I really am, he doesn't want me."

"Yeah, I think I need to have a chat with him." Paul

cracked his knuckles.

"It doesn't matter. Nothing matters now."

"Good to see you haven't lost your flair for the dramatic." Paul merged into traffic. She thought he'd flip around at the light, but he didn't.

"Hello? Your house is in the other direction."

"We're going to Mom and Dad's. I left Carly there to come pick you up. I was going to bring her, but you sounded... rough." He slowed for a light and tapped his fingers on the steering wheel. "You'll feel better once we get home."

"No, I won't. Mom will want to know the details, then she'll give me tips on dating. Possibly suggest a boring, balding guy she could set me up with." Brynn flopped forward and shoved her fingers into her hair. "This is why you don't sleep with the director. Not that I even got to sleep with him, which is just so unfair."

"Okay, my ears are bleeding now," Paul said.

"You don't understand. He hates me, and I've got to go be in a play for five shows where he's inescapable. It's going to be awkward and horrible, with a side of someone shoot me now." The raw achy feeling in her chest grew even bigger. "I love him."

Paul drove the car into Mom and Dad's driveway and sighed. "I'm sorry. I really am."

"Thanks." Brynn flipped the visor and cleaned herself up the best she could. Her eyes were a little red and her makeup was smeary, but it'd have to do.

When she got inside, Carly actually hugged her—so that was what it felt like to be on the other side of an attack hug. "Are you okay?" She looked Brynn up and down. "Wow, great dress. And your hair..." She lifted a couple strands and let it drop. "Whoever the guy is, he's an idiot."

"He's going to be a dead idiot soon," Paul said, wrapping his arm around Carly.

Carly smiled at him. "I admire you for taking care of your sister, but right now, I'm guessing she needs a lot of chocolate, possibly a chick flick—or are you more of a watch-action-or-horror-movies-when-you-have-a-bad-breakup girl?"

"I go for the masochistic, watch romance movies and cry my eyes out while yelling, 'Why can't I find love?'"

Carly laughed. "A girl after my own heart."

For the first time, Brynn saw Carly for who she really was. A beautiful, genuinely nice person who cared about Paul. They'd been on the opposite end of the spectrum in high school, but maybe that was as much Brynn's fault as Carly's. And none of that mattered anymore.

"Girls are weird." Paul kissed Carly's cheek and sighed. "I'll leave you two to find the torturous movie. I'll go see how much chocolate I can dig up."

Brynn walked into the living room and scanned the shelf of DVDs. "Hey, do you remember Dirk Markham?"

Carly wrinkled her nose. "You mean Dirk the Jerk?"

Brynn smiled, though it felt out of place on her face right now. "Yeah. He's still a jerk."

"Is that who you were out with tonight?"

"No! I would never... Just no." Brynn looked at Carly's raised eyebrows and sympathetic expression and thought, *Well, it's not like I've got anything to lose now that Sawyer hates me.* "Remember how I asked you about Sawyer Raines?"

Brynn let loose the mortifying confession, starting with way back in high school, to his showing up at the theater, to the blowup tonight. "So, I'm sure this is super weird for you now, huh?"

Carly patted her hand. "That was such a long time ago. And I'm serious about wishing I knew you better back then—I'm sorry high school sucked so much for you. As for Sawyer... I don't know what I can say except that I'm sorry.

And that he won't ever find anyone better than you. Like, ever, so it's totally his loss."

It still felt like an elephant was standing on her chest, but confessing to Carly had actually lightened the pressure. Brynn might even be the one to initiate the next tackle hug.

Another thing had happened during her confession, as well. She felt like she was finally ready to fully let go of the bitterness she'd held onto over the years. There'd always be guys like Dirk, who only had the glory days of high school, which was sad when she thought about it. Maybe he'd changed, maybe he even had good qualities now, but in the grand scheme of things, it didn't matter. Her old nickname, all her misguided attempts to be cool—even her crush on Sawyer—had formed who she was now. And she liked who she was, even if she'd had to get there the hard way.

She only wished she'd figured that out *before* she'd screwed up everything with Sawyer.

Mom came down the stairs. "Brynn! I didn't know you were here." She hugged her, then studied her, the lines in her forehead deepening. "You look different. And sad. Are you okay?"

Paul came in armed with cookies and a bag of Peanut M&M's. Dad was beside him, a bottle of wine in one hand and a stack of plastic cups in the other. "I hear we're watching a sappy girl movie," he said.

Mom took Brynn's hand in hers, bringing her attention back to her. The question she'd asked still hung in the air unanswered.

Later, Brynn wasn't going to be okay. Right now, she wasn't really either—her heart ached deep down, the kind of throbbing, constant pain that was there to stay. But surrounded by her family and a girl she might just call sister one day, she thought she could maybe get through tonight.

"I'm okay," she lied.

Chapter Seventeen

Brynn doubled over, arms wrapped tightly around her stomach, sure she was going to puke. She was always nervous opening night, but it'd never been this bad. Her insides were revolting, turning on her at the worst possible time. Everyone else was running around, frantic energy in the air. Usually, she'd take in the excitement and let it wash over her. Tonight, it just wasn't enough.

The theater was packed, the buzz of the audience's conversations drifting backstage.

In a lot of ways, though, it felt like only one person was in the place. The guy who hadn't spoken to her and looked away every time she tried to make eye contact. A sharp pain shot through her chest. Last week, every glance, every smile, made her heart soar; today she ached for everything she'd lost.

There was so much to tell him, but no time.

"Brynn, honey, what are you doing?" Wendy approached and tugged on Brynn's dress, smoothing it down in places and fluffing it up in others.

Brynn glanced at Sawyer, who was talking to Leo while gesturing toward the stage. Another stab pierced her heart.

Wendy pulled out a blush compact and swiped the pink across Brynn's cheeks. "What happened with Sawyer?"

"Nothing... He's doing a great job directing."

"That's not what I'm talking about. We all know you've been dating." Wendy gripped Brynn's chin, twisting her face one way and then the other. "You guys are just awful at hiding it."

Hot tears stung her eyes and she blinked quickly—there wasn't time to cry and reapply makeup. "Well, we're not dating anymore."

Wendy sighed. "I was afraid this was going to happen. But you both seemed so happy so I let it go." She studied Brynn, her lips pressed into a tight line. "We need you at your best out there. Are you going to be okay?"

Brynn swallowed her emotions. "The show must go on, right?"

"Right," Wendy said with a decisive nod. "Now let's go touch up your hair."

Her hair was okay last she looked, but she let Wendy lead her to the back room anyway. Once she had enough hairspray on to take out another layer of the ozone, Brynn paced around backstage.

Okay. Focus on the play. Tonight I'm not Brynn McAdams, girl with a shattered heart. I'm Cecily. Girl who believes in love.

She was afraid the audience would see through it. Worse, she was afraid she might burst into tears at any mention of love. Not so great when it was in almost every scene of the play.

Why didn't I choose to be in a show about...zombies or something?

Brynn's dress suddenly felt too tight. She needed the

back taken out a bit or she was going to faint. She went in search of Wendy but ran smack into Sawyer instead.

She tried to step back, but the fake tree was there. Sawyer reached out and caught it as it started to tip, bringing him so close to her she could smell his familiar cologne. Her body reacted automatically, butterflies, heat… She put her hand on his arm.

"Sawyer."

He jerked away. "Don't, Brynn. We can't do this here. Not now."

"Where, then? When?"

He ran his fingers across his brow. "Look, all I want is to do my time and go back to New York."

Razor-sharp panic took hold of her. "You can't just leave. You owe me at least a conversation. A chance to explain everything."

"I don't owe you anything. You can't trap me here."

"I'm not trying to trap you! I thought about coming clean a hundred times. I was so scared of losing you, and scared you'd be mad—I was obviously right about that part. I get it, I broke your trust. But you're not the only one who got hurt, you know. You hurt me in high school."

"I didn't do it on purpose," Sawyer said, his voice still way too cold and angry.

"Yet the result was the same."

Silence fell between them, and a glimmer of hope broke through. *He understands. He's going to give me another chance.*

The muscles in his neck and jaw tightened. "It's like you're not hearing me. I'm leaving. There's no point in trying to fix this. Now get into place; the show is about to start. And make sure no one steps on your skirt. We don't need a wardrobe malfunction tonight."

Everything inside her collapsed. She swallowed past the

lump lodged in her throat. "Now that's how you hurt someone on purpose."

Every time, right before she stepped onstage, Brynn thought, *You're Cecily, a girl who loves with her whole heart and will get her happily ever after.*

She'd made it halfway through by some miracle. The audience was full of the kind of people who added to the energy hanging in the air, transporting them all to a world where stories about liars were charming and love would prevail.

"Oh, don't cough, Earnest," Brynn said, pretending to write in Cecily's journal. "When one is dictating one should speak fluently and not cough. Besides, I don't know how to spell a cough."

Chuckles went through the audience.

Leo moved closer and smiled at her. "Cecily, ever since I first looked upon your wonderful and incomparable beauty, I have dared to love you wildly, passionately, devotedly, hopelessly."

Unexpected longing rose up. That was what a guy was supposed to say. Especially if you'd told him you loved him. She could see Sawyer, sitting there in the front. He didn't love her in any adverb way.

Leo's eyebrows rose.

Right. Brynn shook her head at him. "I don't think that you should tell me that you love me wildly, passionately, devotedly, hopelessly. Hopelessly doesn't seem to make much sense, does it?"

Oh, but it did. Right now, hopelessly in love described her perfectly. She loved someone who'd used her painful memories against her. Crap. The tears were rising again and her throat was so tight she didn't think she'd be able to speak.

Luckily, it was time for Merriman to enter the scene. Brynn clenched her fists. She had to stop thinking about Sawyer and focus. She was about to blow her lines. It'd be a lot easier not to think about him if he wasn't sitting in the first row, looking so damn grumpy.

Her next line she delivered automatically. But she didn't want to phone in her performance. She'd worked hard. And she wasn't going to let everyone down because she'd been let down.

So when it came time for the proposal scene, she peered into Leo's eyes like he was the man of her dreams and put a little extra something behind the kiss.

• • •

Sawyer flinched. He still hated the proposal scene. And as much as he'd been on Brynn and Leo about their lack of chemistry, they pulled it off tonight.

I don't deserve to feel jealous. I was a total asshole earlier. The second the wardrobe malfunction comment slipped out of his mouth, he'd regretted it. Brynn had walked away before he could say he was sorry. He should've gone after her. But then he would've wrapped his arms around her, kissed her, and forgot that he didn't trust her anymore. He could see how she could lie about high school. But the thing with not knowing how to fish? Obviously she was purposely hiding her job from him. Who did that?

How could she even be serious about him if she didn't trust him? He could ask her, only that was the type of conversation two people who wanted to be in a relationship would have. Even if he could forgive Brynn for all the lies, he wasn't going to stick around. He needed to go back to where he belonged. It'd be better for her in the end, anyway.

Man, it was torture to see her up there, though. She'd always shone onstage, but the audience loved her tonight, and she was taking it to a new level. The only time she'd faltered was when she'd looked at him.

I don't think I can survive four more performances. Everyone already knows what they need to do now. Aunt Wendy can take it from here.

And Brynn... He took one last, long look. She'd be okay without him. It was time for both of them to move on before either one of them got hurt.

More hurt, anyway.

Chapter Eighteen

Sawyer disconnected the call with the realtor. Finally, it was all done. With only a couple of hours to spare, too.

"Are you ever going to tell me what's going on?" Mom asked.

Sawyer slid the phone into his pocket. "Everything's done. Sale sign's up in the yard. All the paperwork is finished. I don't think it'll be on the market for long."

"I'm not talking about the house stuff. I'm talking about the girl you were dating. I get the feeling something bad happened." Mom put her hand over his. "Did you two break up?"

Sawyer sighed. "This was why I didn't want to tell you about her in the first place. How come no one listens when I say that I'm not staying here? I'm literally leaving the state in a few hours, with no plans to come back any time soon."

Mom pursed her lips, and he immediately felt guilty. He hadn't meant he would never come see her. He braced himself for the scolding she was about to give him for not planning to visit. "Did she want you to stay?"

Sawyer gritted his teeth, trying to tamp down the traitorous surge of affection that went through him when he thought about Brynn. "It's over, and that's all you need to know. Here's the information on the lake house." He slid the folder to her. "Now, how about I take you to dinner before you drop me at the airport? Somewhere in Charlotte." *Where I won't run into Brynn.*

"Wendy told me about the actress, Sawyer. And I put the clues together between what she said and what you told me. I saw her last night when I went to the show..." Mom raised an eyebrow, not so subtly reminding him that she still didn't approve of his decision to skip the play after opening night. "I didn't realize she was the same girl who worked in the bait shop. Her mom and I had even talked about setting you two up, isn't that funny?"

Hilarious.

"But you found each other by yourselves. Doesn't that seem like fate?"

Realization sparked in his mind. *That's why Brynn didn't want to have dinner with Mom and me. It would've blown her cover.* Every time he tried to make excuses for her lies, he found another one and got mad all over again.

"You're miserable without her, I can see it on your face. You think that kind of love just comes and goes?"

"I don't lo—" A cold knot formed in his gut. He couldn't even say that he didn't love her, as hard as he was trying to lie to Mom. To himself. "It would never work. Now please, please drop it. I'd like to have a nice last night in North Carolina with my mom."

She gave an epic sigh that made it clear how much she wanted to talk about it.

"We'll take off in ten minutes." Sawyer went into his bedroom to finish packing. When he grabbed his deodorant off his dresser, he saw the yearbook.

He opened it up and flipped through the pages until he got to the class list. He ran his fingers down the names until he found Brynn McAdams, then went across to her picture. He'd expected to see her face and suddenly remember. Have a flash of that day she said she'd asked him out.

But he didn't remember the girl smiling from the page. Her hair was light brown and frizzy. The lacy collar of her shirt looked like something she'd wear onstage as part of a costume. Her eyes, her cheeks, her nose—all those features were the same. She was pretty. Maybe not in a stop-traffic kind of way, and she certainly had better control of her hair now, but there was his girl.

Er, not *his* girl.

He sat down on his bed and flipped to the back, where the names were. She was on one other page—the drama club. He flipped to it until he found her. She had her hair up in a bun and her arm was around some gawky-looking dude.

That day backstage when he'd been hammering nails and she'd been painting popped into his head. Right before she'd gotten angry and stormed away, he'd said everyone in his school drama club was a dork. Once again, he felt like a complete ass.

In his defense, this picture didn't exactly scream cool. But still, there was something in Brynn's eyes, the excitement she naturally exuded. Say he wasn't preoccupied at the end of senior year, worried about his parents, trying to help out with his dad and occasionally running away when it got to be too much. Would he have said yes to this girl asking him out? Would he have given her a chance?

He hated himself for it, but probably not. He wouldn't have risked dating a drama geek.

He closed the book and tossed it aside. Again, he was starting to see her side. Why she might hide who she was. But again, it didn't change a thing.

When he came out of his room, Mom was in the hall, fist raised like she was about to knock. She'd changed into a dressy pantsuit and pulled her hair back.

"You look nice," he said.

She smiled. "Thank you. It's not every day I get to go out to dinner with such a handsome companion." She kissed his cheek and he was sure he had a smudge of peach lipstick on there now.

"I'm sorry I haven't been a better son."

"You're the best son a mom could ask for. And I know I keep saying it, but your dad would be proud of you. He really would."

I bet he would've gotten a kick out of Brynn. They could've argued about action movies versus ones with kissing in them. Sawyer tried to shake it off, but he could see her face lit up by the TV screen when they'd watched movies. Remembered the joke she made about his scratchy blanket and how it was fit for a donkey.

He didn't think that had been an act, because what sane person would purposely come up with that? He laughed, and Mom wrinkled her forehead.

"Sorry." He grabbed his suitcase and pulled up the handle so he could wheel it behind him. "Let's get out of here."

. . .

The sign in Sawyer's front yard was the first thing Brynn saw when she parked in front of her house. She got out and stared at it. White with big red letters proclaiming it FOR SALE.

He hadn't come back, not when she was home, anyway. The outside of the house had new siding; the lawn was tidy. Someone else was going to live there, and it would always seem wrong. Brynn wanted to go rip the sign out, but she knew it wouldn't help. She was sure it was listed in computer databases as well. Too bad she didn't know how to hack into that kind of thing.

She trudged up her sidewalk and a spark of silver caught her eye. The porch light she had been sure would come crashing down on her one day was tight against the outside wall, two new screws in the top.

She had no doubt it was Sawyer, but she couldn't figure out why he'd fix it for her.

He hadn't come to the theater since opening night. Brynn had a hard time not getting distracted by his empty seat. She really thought that he'd show up and at least say good-bye, maybe at the wrap party.

But he hadn't shown.

Brynn pulled out her phone, wanting to call Sawyer. She'd wanted to for days, but the fixed porch light gave her the excuse she needed. *Or maybe I should just text a thank-you. That way he'll see it, even if he ignores my call.*

She wondered if he'd flown back to New York already. How could he leave when she still felt so unsettled?

She pushed into her house, fed Lance and Gwen, and then picked up the music box Sawyer had gotten her. She cranked the handle and let the sorrow wash over her with the music. After she and all two of her ex-boyfriends had broken up, she'd felt down for a couple of weeks, and that was even when she *hadn't* been crazy in love with them. One of them she'd even dumped, because she just couldn't stand the thought of faking her way through their relationship anymore. And she *still* had cried and moped around for a week or so.

How long was it going to take to get over Sawyer?

She wasn't sure she'd actually gotten over him the first time, back before she even knew him. Brynn stared at his name on her phone's display until the screen dimmed.

Then she went ahead and hit the call button.

• • •

Sawyer stared at his ringing phone. The girl wasn't very good at taking hints. Mom was browsing the books in the airport newsstand, delaying the moment when they'd have to part ways.

Sawyer stepped outside the store, into the bustle of other passengers getting ready to go through security, saying good-bye to their loved ones. He hit answer and put the phone to his ear. "This needs to stop. Do I really have to change my number?"

"Well, if you'd answer any of my calls or texts," Zoey said, "I wouldn't have to keep calling."

"What is it? Are you pregnant again?"

Her sigh carried over the line. "How many times do I have to apologize? I was desperate for you to talk to me, and I made a mistake. I kept meaning to tell you the truth, but the longer I waited, the harder it got."

Brynn had said the exact same thing. Maybe he was attracted to women who were compulsive liars.

"Believe it or not, I felt awful the entire time," Zoey said. "I actually thought we had a real shot at making it, though, and I... Anyway. This isn't about you and me and how we didn't work out. I met a producer who saw your movie and liked it. He's looking for someone to write a television series that films right here in New York, and wondered if you were interested. I wanted to talk to you before I gave him your number so you'd be prepared. I was about to anyway, since you wouldn't answer, you stubborn ass."

Sawyer scrubbed a hand over his face. "I don't know what your game is this time, Zoey, but I'm not falling for it. You could schedule me a meeting with Scorsese and I still wouldn't get back together with you."

"I don't want to get back together. I'm dating Charles

now."

Charles. It took him a second to remember that was the actor who played the love interest on her TV show.

"And I'm trying to do things differently with him," Zoey continued. "He actually *wants* to be with me. I forgot how nice that was."

Sawyer rolled his eyes.

"This is about the fact that you're a talented guy. You should at least talk to him. I know they're meeting with some other writers this week, though, so you need to get in there soon. I'm having dinner with the producer tomorrow, and I was thinking you should go with me. At least see what he has to say."

Regardless of what she said about moving on, he was still reluctant to believe her. But he'd be in New York tomorrow, so he could swing it. "Fine. I'll talk to them." He rubbed the back of his neck. "Thanks, Zoey."

"Don't mention it. I kind of owed you."

When Sawyer hung up, he saw Brynn had called and left a message. His muscles tensed. If she told him she hated him or that she was still madly in love with him, it'd be like a repeat of the Zoey breakup, and he'd never so much as check out another actress again.

He hit play on the voice mail. "Hey," Brynn said, her smoky voice making his chest tighten. "I noticed you fixed my porch light—anyway, I assume it was you. I just wanted to say thanks. Good luck with everything in New York. Or LA. Whichever you choose, I'm sure I'll be watching one of your movies on the big screen soon."

All the mushy feelings he'd been trying to keep buried came busting out at once. His knees threatened to give way and his heart ached. Brynn was nothing like Zoey. She noticed the little things he'd done for her. She listened when he talked about what he really wanted—only now he wasn't sure. New York didn't seem like home anymore. LA sure as hell didn't sound like home.

All he could see when he tried to picture his future was Brynn's face. And when he forced that image away, he saw himself sitting alone, lonely in the way he'd been before he met her but hadn't even realized he was.

But it was too late—they'd made too big a mess of things, and he was minutes away from boarding a plane. He had a script to write. A meeting with a producer to take. Maybe one day he'd get up the courage to invite Brynn to visit. Once he got some space and figured out a way to talk to her without falling apart, he'd at least call and tell her that he did forgive her for lying to him. That she was a beautiful, kind person, and the guy who ended up with her was going to be one lucky bastard.

That thought sent burning jealousy through his veins. He didn't want to think of the hypothetical lucky bastard making Brynn laugh, putting his arms around her. Kissing her. Building a life with her.

Sawyer closed his eyes for a moment, trying to regain control. He glanced toward the corridor that would take him through security and onto a plane that'd fly him back to his old life. To his tiny, empty apartment equipped with a big TV. That was all he had to look forward to. A TV screen to keep him company.

Shit, shit, shit.

But if I stayed…

He pictured Brynn sitting next to him on a big couch in the living room of the lake house. He could see hints of furniture around them with little knickknacks he never would've picked out himself. He could hear her singing in the shower as he stood in the bathroom, shaving at the sink. If he stretched his mind far enough, he could even see himself and Brynn at the lake with a couple of kids running around.

Learning to fish. Calling him Dad.

He waited for the suffocating sensation that climbed up his body like vines, trying to choke him out, whenever he thought of a life with only one person.

It didn't come.

He even thought of a future that included taking care of Brynn if something happened to her or she got sick. He'd bring her food. He'd carry her from room to room.

He'd do anything for her.

But then he saw himself on the couch, Brynn the one with dark circles under her eyes as she brought *him* food. Helped him down the hall. All her bubbly energy gone, drained from taking care of him. He saw himself as his dad had been at the very end: completely helpless.

It felt like the bottom of his stomach had dropped out.

He reminded himself that the doctors had told him it was unlikely he'd have the same disease. Unlikely. Not impossible. And he couldn't do that to Brynn. It'd kill him to break her spirit like that. Mom might not regret it after being married to Dad for so long, but if Dad could've spared her the pain altogether, Sawyer had a feeling he would've done it. He'd practically said as much one afternoon when they were watching movies together.

"Look at me, son," he'd said. "Here I lie, as helpless as a baby. I'm not a partner to your mother anymore, I'm a burden. I wish I could've spared her all this..." Dad had put his hand over Sawyer's, his frail fingers barely able to squeeze. "I wish I could've spared you both. But man, you guys made it worth it. It might've been shorter than most, but I've had a good life."

A hand touched his arm. "Sawyer? Are you okay?"

He blinked at the wetness threatening to form in his eyes and then looked down at his mom. He tried to open his mouth to answer but had to clear his throat first. "I think I better go through security, just in case it takes longer than usual."

Mom nodded. "Okay. Be careful, and thanks for everything." She hugged him tightly and placed another peach-lipstick kiss on his cheek—the same spot he'd had to clean off at the restaurant earlier. She started to pull back, but then clamped her hand onto his arm. "I can't let you go before telling you one last thing…"

Sawyer automatically tensed, sure she was making a final Hail-Mary-Pass attempt to get him to stay.

"When I was in that fishing shop and that beautiful girl was helping me," Mom said, "I told her I had an amazing son; I was trying to get her to go meet you at the coffee shop."

"Mom, I told you I don't want to talk a—"

"You let me finish, Sawyer Nathaniel Raines." She hadn't used all three of his names since high school, and it surprised him enough to snap his mouth closed. "She said she was dating someone, and when I pushed, she told me she loved him. Said it with such passion and conviction I knew there was no talking her out of it."

They stared at each other for a moment, his mom obviously wanting to make sure it sank in, at the same time that he was doing his best not to.

"'Bye, Ma."

He glanced out the front glass doors of the airport, where he could still see a hint of North Carolina in the distance.

'Bye, Brynn.

Chapter Nineteen

Three weeks had passed since Brynn had stood on this very stage, playing Cecily, a girl who believed in romance and wrote herself love letters from Earnest.

And Sawyer had sat right where the current director was— Brynn still felt hollow inside whenever she thought of Sawyer Raines. Only it was the kind of hollow that accentuated the emptiness, making everything from her neck to her stomach radiate pain.

Even when he was gone, he managed to ruin the place she always used to escape reality.

She delivered her monologue from *Kiss Me Kate* and then exited the stage. Usually she'd stick around and hear the other actors audition. Wave at familiar faces. Wish them luck.

Lately, she thought that luck was crap. It certainly hadn't done her any favors.

Anyway, she had an engagement party to get to. Brynn still couldn't believe Paul had asked Carly to marry him. When he'd mentioned he was thinking about it at the beginning of the week, Brynn tried to hint that it was a little fast—for the record, it was a *lot* fast—and that he might want to give it another couple of months to make sure it was right.

Things between them had been chilly since. But he'd proposed and Carly had said yes. Yay for love. Or something like that.

Brynn pulled her car up to her parents', forced her lips into a smile, and walked through the front door. The house was filled with people, several she didn't even recognize. When she spotted Dani and Wes in the crowd, she made a beeline for them.

She hugged Dani, and went ahead and hugged Wes, too.

"How you holding up?" Dani asked.

"I could use a drink. A strong one."

"On it," Wes said. Brynn was going to tell him that she could get it, but he was already pushing through the crowd of people.

There was a big banner hanging on the archway that said Congrats! Brynn could just make out her brother and his new fiancée standing underneath it. She waited for the contact love-high. But she got nothing.

Dani leaned her hip on the wall next to Brynn. "So, this isn't a setup, I swear, but turns out Paul knows Connor, and he happens to be here right now."

It took Brynn a few seconds to realize who that even was. "The cop?"

Dani nodded, then surreptitiously pointed to a tall, muscled guy with dark hair. "So? What do you think?"

Brynn was pretty sure her eyebrows were as high as they could go. "I think I said that I don't go for jocks, and that guy looks like he eats jocks for breakfast."

Dani laughed. "Well, I can still introduce you…see if you hit it off?"

Brynn thought about it for a second. "Seriously, he's so handsome and ripped it's almost hard to look directly at him, much less figure out something to say." Brynn turned to face Dani, the familiar ache between her ribs deepening. "But really, my heart's just not in it."

"I understand," Dani said. "Plus, the more I'm around him, the more I think he's a bit of a player, anyway. Probably not a good thing for you." One of her dark eyebrows quirked up. "Unless…you want a hot rebound guy to make you forget everything for a little while?"

It was one of those things that sounded good in theory, but Brynn knew she could never go through with it. The truth was, she wasn't even tempted. She was pretty sure Sawyer had ruined her for other men forever.

Before she even answered, Dani put her hand on Brynn's shoulder. "Someday you'll be ready to move on, and we'll find someone perfect for you when you are."

Brynn nodded like that was a possibility. Wes came back with drinks and Brynn wasted no time starting on hers. Wes wrapped his arms around Dani and brushed his stubbled face across her neck, making her laugh.

Still no love-high. The butterflies were obviously dead now. Not even dormant. Sawyer had plucked off their wings and tossed them aside, just like he had her. Brynn stared into her glass. "I think I'm too dramatically depressed to be here." She took a large swig of the fruity drink, thinking it wasn't nearly strong enough, whatever it was. Then Brynn noticed Paul and Carly circling the room, giant grins on their faces, and decided she should go say hi to the newly engaged couple.

"Brynn!" Carly threw her arms around Brynn with such force she nearly tipped over. "Can you believe it?"

"I'm so happy for you." Brynn glanced at her brother. "Both of you."

One of Carly's family members came over, so Brynn and Paul scooted off to the side. "I meant what I said about being happy for you," Brynn said. "It just took me by surprise."

"I know. And I know you're still hurting from your breakup." Paul met her eyes, his expression serious. "I thought I was helping, giving you that advice about holding back. But I think I just screwed you up."

"Oh, I managed to do that all by myself."

"Still. I feel bad. I know a thing or two about bad breakups, and you do get over it eventually. You'll find someone else. Trust me."

That seemed to be the popular opinion tonight, but she still didn't believe it. Tears were rising, threatening to make an appearance. She didn't know if she would find someone else. Right now, she didn't even know if she wanted to. How could she risk her heart again if it could get beat up this badly?

Deep down, though, she knew he was right. Someday, she might be ready to move on.

Just not today.

Probably not for a long time.

• • •

Sawyer slung his laptop bag over his shoulder. He'd just sent his new script to his agent. He'd practically rewritten it all in the past few weeks, but it was the best thing he'd ever written, if he did say so himself.

Considering all he could see when he wrote the female love interest was Brynn, it was as addicting as it was torturous to work on. Tomorrow, he was meeting again with the producers Zoey had set him up with. Really, he felt like the job was his, all he had to do was say yes. But did he want to write for television? It was a different format, but he knew he could do it if he threw himself into it.

His ringing phone interrupted his thoughts. He studied the unfamiliar number and then decided to answer. "Hello?"

"Hi, Sawyer, it's Patricia. I called to tell you about the

multiple offers we've gotten on the house."

He wasn't sure why the realtor was talking to him about it. "You need to call my mom. She's the one who's going to decide."

"I did, but she told me to try you."

Sawyer sighed. Why would she do that? He knew the answer, of course. She thought he'd change his mind. He thought of the house he'd put so much work into and grown to love. Of Brynn watching movies with him on the floor. Painting the kitchen.

He almost wanted to keep it as a souvenir of their time together. One hell of a huge, expensive souvenir.

When Patricia told him more about the offers, his jaw almost hit the filthy sidewalk. "Well, obviously let's go with the highest bid."

"Escrow would be sixty days on that one. The other one is a little less, but we can close in thirty. Something to think about."

Sawyer glanced up in time to see he'd somehow ended up right next to a theater. This area of town was filled with them, so that wasn't a shock. The poster advertising *The Importance of Being Earnest* was, though. And the fact that Brynn was staring at him from the poster.

His heart gave a couple fast thuds and he stood there, frozen. On closer look, though, it wasn't Brynn at all. Just another actress with dark hair.

"Mr. Raines? Do you want to accept their offer?"

• • •

Brynn was seconds from freedom when Mom called her name.

"Leaving already?" Mom asked, in that tone that meant you really shouldn't be. It'd been three hours. Most of the guests had come and gone. Only the family members and closest friends remained, most sloppy drunk by now.

Brynn dropped her hand from the doorknob and cursed under her breath. "I need to get home."

"Are you not sleeping well? You look tired."

Brynn ran a hand through her hair. Why did people think they sounded considerate when they said you looked tired? Really it was just another way of saying you look like hell. But when Brynn turned around, she could see the genuine concern on Mom's face.

"I was hoping we'd get a chance to talk," Mom said.

Other family members, both theirs and Carly's, were the only people left, but it'd be easier to have a real talk away from everyone. "Outside on the porch?"

Mom glanced at her living room, and Brynn knew she was going to say she needed to host. But then she smiled. "Sure."

They settled onto the porch swing, and for a moment, they simply sat, enjoying the quiet.

"It's funny," Mom said. "Most people are stressed at the thought of a wedding. But I'm actually excited because it'll give me something to do."

Brynn stopped swinging and tucked her leg up, trying to figure out how to respond to that. Before she could, Mom waved a hand through the air. "I know I call too much, and I come into the store more than I need to. I've probably been driving you and your brother mad. I've just been...bored. I thought I'd retire from the shop and do all the things I never had time to do before. Then I did a bunch of them and found that I hadn't missed out on much."

"Why don't you go fishing with Dad, then?" It scared Brynn to put it out there, but after fishing with Dad, she'd wanted to ask, and now seemed as good a time as any to face the truth head on. She hoped.

"It's just that… He and I are together. All. Day. Long. I know that sounds horrible—I should *want* to spend that much time with him, right? We used to work together every day, and I loved that. But we were busy with customers and running numbers and orders, and…well…life. Now we say everything we've got to say, and by the end of the day, we don't have anything new to talk about. If I let him go fishing alone, and I do something else, we can come together and talk again."

Brynn took a moment to let that sink in. "I guess I thought that once you found the one, you'd want to spend every waking second together."

"Maybe some couples can handle that. But I think it's good to have hobbies separate from each other. You want to find a guy who likes a lot of things you do, but also likes a few of the things you don't."

Brynn thought of Sawyer and his action movies. And when she remembered how they'd both been in high school— they couldn't have been more different.

She really needed to stop thinking about him, though.

"Are you hurting over whatever happened between you and Judith Raines's son?"

Brynn jerked her head up.

"It's written all over your face." Mom swept Brynn's hair behind her ear. "I've tried not to push, but I'm worried about you."

For the second time that night, Brynn was fighting tears. "I thought he was the one. But he didn't want me."

Mom pulled her into a hug. "Well, what an idiot."

Brynn laughed. "It was me, too. I screwed up. I thought I had to hide who I was to be good enough for him."

"I used to worry about you," Mom said. "That you had your head in the clouds too much. But you're a strong girl. And now I think more people should have their heads in the clouds. Don't ever change, okay?"

"Okay."

"And once you're ready, I know a cute dentist."

Brynn couldn't help but laugh. Apparently Mom wasn't going to change, either. "Let's set up a weekly girls' night. Dancing, or we can go to Charlotte and see what trouble we can get ourselves into? Something crazy enough to give you a few stories to tell Dad."

Mom smiled. "I'd love that. And just so you know, your dad wants to get you out on the water again. Maybe you can indulge him sometimes, too."

"I will if you will."

"Deal," Mom said.

Dad poked his head out the door. "There you two are. I can't find the extra bottles of wine."

Mom stood. "I'll come help you find them."

Dad extended his hand and Mom took it.

Then it happened. A tiny spark of hope lit inside Brynn that all wasn't lost. When you loved someone, you worked at it. Fought for it.

Maybe she hadn't fought hard enough for Sawyer. And if it took her going all the way to New York to get him to give her another chance, she was going to do it.

Chapter Twenty

Brynn thought she'd feel better once she got out on the water. After she'd shot death glares at a customer for asking her to take all the lures down so he could see them better, Paul decided she needed the rest of the day off before she strangled someone. He'd given her the spare key to Dad's boat and pointed toward the lake. Suddenly all that water looked like the perfect escape.

So she'd driven the boat out until the buildings along the shore were tiny squares and the breeze was whipping her hair around her face. She'd even baited a pole and set it up, though she was staring through it more than at it.

While at least she felt less like inflicting bodily harm, irritation was still coursing through her veins. Maybe it was the looming dark clouds overhead, or maybe it was the way time had slowed to a slug crawl.

Or maybe it was because she'd wanted to scream/cry/throw things ever since she noticed the For Sale sign in the yard next door had been taken down. Actually, there was no maybe about it.

She'd told herself it was okay. That it didn't change anything. She was still going to find a way to show Sawyer how much she missed him; she just needed to figure out how she was going to pull it off. Showing up on his doorstep in New York seemed like a total stalker move, but she hadn't ruled it out.

She could try calling again, but somehow it didn't seem like enough—there was no way she could truly express how sorry she was about everything, or how much she wanted him to give her another shot. Even if they had to date long distance. At this point, she was considering telling him she wouldn't mind if he dated other people on the side if he wanted to.

But that would be a lie, and probably not the best way to start fresh with Sawyer.

Still, that missing For Sale sign hung over her, making her feel like she was too late.

A drop of water hit her nose and then her cheek. She looked up, the falling raindrops shining in the rays of sunlight trying to break through the gray sky. The breeze picked up and the dark clouds shifted, covering the sun.

Dad always swore rain brought out the fish. Brynn didn't know about that, but as long as it didn't get too heavy, she enjoyed the occasional rainstorm. How it would cool off the hot summer afternoon and make everything smell fresh and clean. The way the raindrops would make little ripples across the surface of the water.

Thunder rolled in the distance and the air shifted, as if the storm was only getting started. A little rain was okay, but if it got too heavy, she could get cold. Plus, if lightning started up, well, she was one of the tallest things on the lake, so there was also that to worry about.

To stay or not to stay. That is the question.

How much more time did she need on the lake? She

thought of having to look out her window at Sawyer's now-sold house, and decided maybe she'd live here instead of going back and seeing someone else moving in. More drops fell, faster and faster, the water starting to seep into her clothes.

The motor of a boat buzzed in the distance, growing louder by the second. Brynn glanced toward it, blinking at the water sticking to her eyelashes. Common courtesy said to keep generous space between boats, but this one was driving right at her.

It's going to stop before barreling into me, right? Her pulse quickened. *Unless the driver can't see me through the rain.*

The boat slowed and banked last minute, the waves rocking her enough she had to grip onto the railing.

"Brynn? Is that you?"

She recognized the voice before she could make out Sawyer's features. Goose bumps broke out across her skin and she could hear her rising pulse pounding in her ears. She put her hand over her eyes to block the rain and squinted, needing visual confirmation before her emotions skyrocketed completely out of control. Sawyer's dark hair was slightly damp, his cheeks reddened from the wind—but it was him.

"Thank goodness," he said, moving toward her. "I went by the shop and your brother told me you were out here. I've been searching every green boat on this lake. There're more than you'd expect."

Some time between realizing it was him and trying to make sense of his words, Brynn's heart had stopped beating.

"Also, there wasn't anyone manning the rental place when I got there, but the keys were in this boat, so...let's just say I borrowed it, and people *might* be looking for me soon." Sawyer got up onto the edge of the boat. "But I had to find you, and I couldn't wait another second. Brynn..." Sawyer took a large step, starting across to her boat. But it rocked and his foot slipped on the wet siding. She watched in shock as he fell into the lake with a loud splash.

"Sawyer!" She dropped down to her knees and leaned over the edge.

His head broke the surface of the water. He shook out his hair and shot her a sheepish grin. "That went differently in my head."

She couldn't help but smile at that, despite the ball of nerves twisting in her gut. It was the story of her life, everything going differently—and more disastrously—than she'd planned. As he swam to the edge of the boat and climbed on, her heart started beating again, faster and faster, like it was trying to make up for all the beats it'd missed.

And then he was standing in front of her. His hair was plastered to his head and water ran down his face in rivulets, clumping his eyelashes together. His shirt was molded to every sexy inch of his torso, and she wasn't sure if she should laugh or cry or throw her arms around him and beg him never to leave her again.

Sawyer reached out and cupped her cheek. "Maybe I didn't see you in high school, Brynn McAdams…but now you're all I see, everywhere I look." He took another step closer, until their chests met, rising and falling against each other, so close not even the rain could get between them. "I'm sorry I was too scared to stay before. But I'm going to try to fix it."

"I was about ready to come to New York and bang down your door," Brynn said. "I just…didn't know where it was."

One corner of his mouth twisted up. "Well, now all you have to do is walk a few steps from your place to mine. Bang down my door any time you want."

He didn't sell the house! Sweet relief flooded her, and the sense of wrongness that'd been plaguing her since she saw the missing sale sign lifted. Brynn placed her hands on the sides of his waist. "I'm sorry I didn't tell you the truth, but I was afraid once I did, you wouldn't want the real me."

"I was afraid to admit that I might need another person, so I guess that makes us even."

"Just to be on the safe side, there are some things you should probably know…" She peered into his green eyes. "I know enough about fishing to write one of those 'For Dummies' books on it."

Sawyer slid his hand from her cheek to her neck and stroked his thumb across her jaw. "Good. I plan to do a lot of fishing now that I live here."

"And I randomly break into song, and often quote lines from classic literature and plays in normal conversations."

"I need more culture in my life. Plus, I think it's adorable when you do that." Another brush of his thumb, and her breath grew shallow.

She licked her lips, trying to focus, needing to get it all out. "I have seven kissing figurines and I'm obsessed with love stories and the reason my birds are named Lance and Guinevere is because I always wanted those two to find a way to be together."

Sawyer smiled down at her and her heart rate rose impossibly high, making her dizzy. "Who doesn't love a sweeping bird romance?"

Warmth flooded her body, affection and attraction all at the same time. Now for the hard part—the part that replaced her momentary happiness with a sharp ache. "In high school I was in drama club, dressed weird, and obsessed over a cute boy I didn't even know."

Sawyer lowered his head and brushed his lips against hers. "Lucky boy."

A tight band formed around her chest. "And in my only school play appearance, one of the actors stepped on my skirt and the entire school saw my underwear. It was awful."

"I'm sorry that happened to you. But if it makes you feel

any better…" He placed a kiss on the sensitive spot just under her ear. "I'm dying to see you in your underwear."

A laugh escaped her lips.

Sawyer rested his forehead against hers, the wet from his clothes seeping into hers and further soaking her, but she didn't care. She wrapped her arms around his waist and held on tighter.

"I have a couple of confessions, too," Sawyer said. "In high school, a beautiful, unique girl apparently asked me out. And I was dumb enough not to say yes. Now, I could make the excuse that I was lost, unable to think about anything except how my dad was going to die—and it'd be the truth. But that girl didn't deserve to be treated like that. And later, when I got lucky enough for that girl to give me another chance and she told me she loved me, I freaked out…"

He locked eyes with her. "I've missed you so much. Not the fake girl, but the one who sang while she painted, teased me about liking grape soda, and got up onstage and threw herself into a part so much that I got lost in the story. That's the girl I fell for. That's the girl I'm in love with."

Tingly butterflies swarmed her stomach and a euphoric buzz flooded her from head to toe. "I love you, too."

Time slowed, each raindrop falling from the sky glittering around them. Then he pulled her flush against him and captured her mouth with his. It was a blur of lips and tongues, hands sliding over her body, the feel of his skin under her fingertips. The taste of fresh rain in his kiss, the cool water pouring from the sky combating the heat rising through her body.

She sucked his lower lip between hers and smiled when he groaned.

Sawyer had come back for her.

He loved her.

And surprisingly enough, the romance stories she'd always loved so much didn't have nothin' on the real thing.

Epilogue

Sawyer kept typing a sentence or two, and then glancing at Brynn. Another sentence. Brynn. She'd said she didn't mind if he worked on his computer in bed—that she had a novel to keep her busy. Only all he could think about was keeping her busy in other ways. They'd made good use of his new bedroom furniture—an antique oak set that had made Brynn's eyes light up when she saw it in the store. She'd gotten so excited picking it out, he'd told her she could be in charge of decorating the master bedroom. It was now the perfect blend of his style and hers, and his new favorite room in the house.

A whole month had passed since he'd officially moved from New York, and life just got better and better. His agent had sold his new screenplay—and they were actually filming the movie in Wilmington, where he was going to try his hand at directing. It might crash and burn, but Brynn was on board, telling him he could do it, and that made him feel like he could. Well, that, and it made him love her even more, which he'd thought was impossible. Yet every day, he did.

He typed another sentence, stared at the blinking cursor for a couple of beats...and then closed his laptop. Brynn glanced over the top of her reading glasses at him, and his heart rate kicked up several notches. He set his computer on the nightstand and then leaned over and kissed Brynn's shoulder.

She raised an eyebrow. "You told me I needed to hold you off until you got your pages done, and I know you didn't get them written in fifteen minutes."

"I didn't realize you'd be so distracting," he mumbled against her skin. "I'll get to the writing later."

"No, you told me if you said that, I should use sex to motivate you." She shrugged her shoulder, bumping him off it. "So open up that computer and get your pages done. And *then* you'll get your reward."

He moved his lips to her neck, smiling when he heard her sharp intake of breath. "You know what I was thinking?"

She tilted her head back, allowing him better access. "That you're going to blame me later when you don't have your work done?"

He kissed his way across her jaw. "Besides that."

Brynn took off her glasses and set them on the side table—she was giving in. When she turned back to him, she ran her fingers through his hair, managing to turn him on even more than he had been seconds ago. She pressed her lips lightly to his. "What were you thinking?"

Thoughts were getting fuzzy, and it took him a moment to realize he'd started a conversation. "I was thinking that you go nicely in my bed."

She pushed him back. He was about to complain, but then she straddled him, her nightgown sliding up so that her bare thighs were against his. Her dark hair hung around them like a curtain. "I'm an accessory now?"

He grinned. "A really sexy accessory. And I was kind of

wondering…" He slid his hands up the smooth skin of her thighs, gathering the silky fabric in his hands. "If you wanted to be a permanent one."

She jerked upright, her eyes going wide. "Are you saying what I think you're saying?"

He propped himself up on his elbows. "Move in with me."

The heat running through his body cooled a bit. Maybe this wasn't the best time to ask a question like that. Hell, he didn't know how to do it. He'd just thought it and blurted it out. Maybe Brynn wanted something more planned out. More romantic.

But then the most beautiful smile he'd ever seen curved her lips, easing his worries. "You think you can handle me full time?"

"Hell yeah."

"Okay. Let's do it."

It was like the last piece inside him clicked into place. He felt whole in a way he hadn't in years, and he saw that image he'd been envisioning a while ago, with he and Brynn and a couple of kids. He could see a future, and instead of wanting to run from it, he wanted to hold on tight.

Brynn slipped her hands under his T-shirt, tugging it up over his head. Then her soft lips came down on his. "You were right," she said, her voice breathy. "Work can definitely wait."

Acknowledgments

Thanks to my husband and children, who were supportive all through this book, from the brainstorming through the writing and editing and panicking and burning of dinners. Yeah, that was pretty crazy, but we survived, so yay! Thanks to my sisters Randa and April, who listened to me as I ran a hundred ideas by them trying to get this book right, and assured me I could write it, even when I doubted it. Super huge thanks to my sister-in-law, Crystal Vaughn, for her knowledge about putting on plays, and for answering my MANY texts, e-mails, and phone calls. And for being the kind of girl who is brave enough to get onstage. To my critique group, Julia Allen, Brandy Vallance, and Bob Spiller, for looking at large chunks at a time and telling me I was on the right track and that you laughed in all the right places. And more than that, for being amazing friends.

I also got encouragement from Jennifer Probst, Lisa Burstein, Rachel Harris (another brainstormer in crime), and Karen Erickson along the way. And as always, thanks to Anne Eliot, who had to endure many frantic phone calls and always found a way to bring it back to the magical elixir. What would I do without you, my friend? You and I, we're the same.

My editors, Stacy Abrams and Alycia Tornetta, make me a better writer, and on top of being good at their jobs, are a total blast to hang out with! Thanks to my amazing support team at Entangled, editors, publicists, writers—you all rock! I'd be lost without my publicity team, Heather Riccio, the publicist ninja, the fabulous Jessica Turner, and Elana Johnson.

To my girls in the Time Zones Will Not Defeat Us Club, huge hugs! You make me feel like a rock star, and it's so nice to have a place to chat books and so much more. To my parents, who've always been there for me. Thanks to my brother, Greg, for fixing everything in my house that fell apart so I could ignore it and keep writing. I've got an amazing support system of family and friends, including my extended family and the amazing one I married in to. To all the bloggers who've read and reviewed my books, I appreciate it so much! Special shout-out to Andrea Thompson, who always keeps me entertained on Twitter. 3DG forever, glad we don't have to sob anymore.

And to anyone who's read my books—THANK YOU! Because of you, I get to keep doing the best job in the world.

About the Author

Cindi Madsen is a *USA Today* bestselling author of contemporary romance and young adult novels. She sits at her computer every chance she gets, plotting, revising, and falling in love with her characters. Sometimes it makes her a crazy person. Without it, she'd be even crazier. She has way too many shoes, but can always find a reason to buy a pretty new pair, especially if they're sparkly, colorful, or super tall. She loves music and dancing and wishes summer lasted all year long. She lives in Colorado (where summer is most definitely NOT all year long) with her husband, three children, an overly-dramatic tomcat, & an adorable one-eyed kitty named Agent Fury.

You can visit Cindi at: www.cindimadsen.com, where you can sign up for her newsletter to get all the up-to-date information on her books.

Follow her on Twitter @cindimadsen.

Find your Bliss with these great releases...

DATING THE WRONG MR. RIGHT
a *Sisters of Wishing Bridge* novel by Amanda Ashby

Ben Cooper is doing his best to build his business and help his parents. The last thing he needs is the distraction that is Pepper Watson. She's prickly every time he's in her presence, but he sees another side of her. And kissing her is pretty much the best thing that's ever happened to him. He's putting down roots. She's running away. It's going to take more than a wish for these two to find their happily ever after.

THE BAD BOY NEXT DOOR
a *Kendrick Place* novel by Jody Holford

Shay Matthews moved to Boston for a fresh start...new apartment, new job, new routine. After too many years being coddled by her overbearing older brothers, Shay's ready for some freedom and maybe a nice, easygoing guy. She wasn't expecting to literally run into the scowling, brooding, (and unfairly smoking hot) guy next door. But the more Shay tries to convince herself that her sweet building manager, Brady, is the guy for her, the more Mr. Completely Wrong-for-Her Wyatt invades her mind and her heart.

FALLING FOR HER ENEMY
a *Still Harbor* novel by Victoria James

Alex McAllister always dreamed of a life filled with family, but being abandoned at a young age left her wary of letting anyone in. Now that she's settled in Still Harbor, Alex is faced with the magnetic pull of Hayden Brooks, the handsome workaholic who claims he's the biological father of her adopted daughter. A paternity test is all that's standing between Alex and her dream, but Hayden's about to make the most shocking decision of his life, just in time for Christmas…

LOVE HIM OR LEAVE HIM
a *Small Town, Big Love* novel by Sara Daniel

Connor O'Malley and Becca Sanders were once high school sweethearts, ripped apart by rumors in their small town. Connor left to join the military, and Becca stayed, waiting for her younger brother to graduate so she could live her dreams of traveling the world. But now that Connor's back as the town sheriff, Becca finds herself struggling to resist the too-handsome man who broke her heart.

Made in the USA
Monee, IL
14 September 2020